Self-published first edition, Sept 2014.

ISBN-13: 978-1500643942

ISBN-10: 1500643947

Copyright © Steve Richards 2014.

The right of Steve Richards to be identified as the author of this work is in accordance with the Copyright Designs and Patents Act, 1988.

This book is a work of fiction. Names, characters, places and incidents are products of the author's warped imagination or are used fictitiously. Any resemblances to locales, events or persons, living or dead, is entirely coincidental. (I mean, you've gotta be a sick bastard to believe any of this stuff, especially the shit that goes down on page 127. That's fucked up.)

All rights reserved. No part of this publication may be reproduced, stored in or introduced into any retrieval system or transmitted in any form or by any means (digitally, traced with crayons or smuggled into a castle eyrie by carrier pigeon etc.) without the prior written approval of the author. If you do, I'll set Seamus on you.

Cover artwork is copyright of Paul Salisbury at Koopdesign.co.uk

The moral right of the author has been asserted. (No idea what this means but saw it in the small print on another book so thought I'd include it here. Why not, eh? It's a free fucking country.)

Dedicated to Dave Richards (1936-2002).

Father, grandfather, husband and posthumous and perpetual President of The DRMT, golf's fifth major.

Preface

I've never been much of a dreamer.

Not to say I don't have the odd mental musing about playing golf at Augusta National one day or holding out hope that Israelis and Palestinians might finally embrace and play cards over strong coffee.

No, what I mean is that I don't have proper dreams. You know, when you inhabit that hazy hinterland between sleep and consciousness.

In my whole 44 years to date of slumber, I reckon I've had a grand total of ten dreams I've been able to recall.

Most of those in recent decades, I'll admit, seem to have involved Charlton Athletic beating Crystal Palace in the FA Cup Final with the winning goal scored by Bill Murray in full Ghostbusters garb.

Then one night in 2012, I had one such apparition that involved neither.

What it did contain, however, was all the detail in the story you're just about to read - the full shebang; the plot, the characters, the twists and turns and even some of the swearing. The only disappointment was that I woke up just before the denouement revealed itself. It was the most exhilarating dream I've ever had or am ever likely to have. When I awoke, I wrote down all of the detail I could remember and then did nothing with it until I bought myself an iPad mini in early 2014 and started to write up the story while commuting in and out of Glasgow.

The writing process has been hugely cathartic so I'm not really that fussed if you like the book or not.

Of course that's total bollocks. I'd love you to love it and recommend it to your mates.

Finally, thanks to the effortlessly talented Paulo 'Maldinus' Salisbury for designing the book cover and to my long-suffering wife, Fiona, for encouraging me to finally put fingertips to keyboard. Thanks also to my

SUNSET OVER SUNSET © Steve Richards

reviewers: Spax, Walt, Mart, Batesy, Sam and Andy.

And if you're a bloke that has ever been away on a business trip, beware.

This really could happen to you...

(PS Sorry, mum, for all the swearing)

1
Going for a Song

"Jeysus sufferin' Christ, Seamus. You're some piece o' work."

"Leave him," said Donal, "you know it's his thing. Let him get on wi' it and we can get the feck outta here."

Seamus approached the quivering man. He was bound to an office swivel chair with gaffer tape, hands behind him. In his mouth was a tennis ball. Calmly, Seamus put the canvas holder onto the small table and unfurled it to reveal a row of gleaming surgical instruments.

The man in the chair's eyes bulged. He was straining his neck to get a better view but the thick black tape wound around his forehead pressed his head against the back of the chair, restricting his range of vision.

Slowly and deliberately, Seamus perused his instruments while putting on his surgical gloves and mask. Carefully, he selected one of the scalpels. Without making eye contact with his victim, he reached over to the man's arm, unfastened his sleeve and rolled up his pale blue shirt. The man let out a low-pitched shriek, muffled by the furry, yellow ball squashed into his mouth.

Seamus looked down, towards the man's crotch. The man immediately stopped convulsing. Sweat poured from his brow, matting his short, wispy hair. Unhurried, Seamus then pointed the scalpel towards the man's lap. The man closed his eyes. He started to whimper, shaking his head from side to side, as much as his binds would allow.

From a distance of ten metres, Seamus's colleagues stood and watched. They were intrigued. They were watching a skilled professional going about his business. One of the three glanced at his watch. The youngest pulled a set of car keys from his pocket and shook them impatiently.

Seamus swung his head around and fixed his gaze on the young man. Even from that distance, Seamus's stare seemed to paralyse him.

Everybody froze, silently still, even the man bound to the chair.

Seamus held his stare for a further five seconds before turning his head slowly back towards his quarry. He reached down and cut a precise line into the man's jeans, along the inside of his inner thigh. He then made another deft cut at a right-angle and then another to form three sides of a square. He pulled the flap of denim open.

Still stooping, he turned his head back towards his colleagues.

"Change?" he barked through his surgical mask. One of the men held up a silver coin.

"iPod?" he called sharply.

The tallest of the three bent down and picked up an iPod. Seamus straightened his back so his head was alongside the man in the chair. He leant in so the mask covering his mouth was almost touching the man's left ear. He spoke in a deep-pitched steady voice with a strong Dublin accent.

"Ok, bigman. The key thing to remember is not to panic. Everything has been taken care of. I am a meticulous man. Relax and try to enjoy the music. *Harold Melvin and the Blue Notes*. Great track."

The moment the final word was uttered, Seamus quickly reached down to the man's arm and made a 10cm vertical incision. Without pause he then placed his scalpel into the man's lap, placed the blade through the flap in the denim and with an expert flick of the wrist, made a deep and effortless cut through the flesh to slice through the artery.

Seamus nodded to his henchman who turned on the track on the iPod and, unhurried, wiped the scalpel blade with a crimson handkerchief and returned it to its designated place. Without looking at his victim, who was by now bleeding profusely from his two wounds and staring in bemused panic, he walked toward the exit.

Music muffled his footsteps. And Harold Melvin sang, 'Don't leave me this way…"

SUNSET OVER SUNSET © Steve Richards

2
Come Fly With Me

"Bored, bored, bored, bored, bored," Craig said. Although not out loud. That would've earned him a scowl. Or even a tut. Or maybe even a scowl and a series of tuts.

Anita, his wife of eight years was changing the duvet cover of the double bed in their two bedroom bungalow in Corstorphine, just to the west of Edinburgh. What newlywed couple buys a bungalow? Craig had wanted the one bedroom flat in the city centre: High ceilings, sash windows, cornicing and two minutes' walk to a pub next to the kebab shop. But, as usual, sense had prevailed. For 'sense', read 'Anita'.

They had met in London while both were working as graduate trainees. Two Scots in a foreign land, thrust together by fate and several double vodkas. Craig's head had been turned by the lilt of a familiar accent, floating across the hubbub of the packed pub in London's financial district. They chatted. He teased. He joked. He bought more vodka. And, perhaps most notably, she later took her pants off.

Anita was mortified. But Craig was smitten. The whole London thing had been part of his training at the solicitors firm to which he had blindly applied. After three assessment centres, largely spent larking about, the firm had signed both of them up. 'A free spirit,' one assessor had scribbled alongside his name. Another disagreed, preferring 'prone to distraction and unconventional in thought and deed.'

Prophetic words indeed as, the very next evening, Craig's unconventional thought was to have a fire extinguisher fight with his fellow trainees in their five-star lodgings, a deed that almost got him thrown off the programme.

Anita and Craig had embraced their coupledom with the gusto of two carefree twentysomethings with money to burn in The Big Smoke. After only six months of making each other's acquaintance, they moved in together in a poky flat in Islington. Craig had switched from the solicitors to pursue a path of lesser resistance, in the marketing sector. No more stuffy suits. No more stifling compliance and regulation. Free spirited unconventional thinking was actively encouraged in the marketing industry. Silliness was applauded. And even better, they paid you more and you went out for drinks in the daytime. Craig had found his calling.

Anita was a very different animal. She stuck at it. Her meticulous nature, eye for detail not to mention her sassy dress-sense had turned heads. These heads, in particular, tended to belong to males in their early fifties. Her professional performance was exemplary. She effortlessly garnered the respect of older, more experienced co-workers and she was promoted three times in two years. She was going places and began to out-earn her husband which provided a license to call the shots on the domestic front. Anita chose the car. Anita chose the summer holiday. And Anita chose the bungalow back in their native Scotland, where they moved after the initial lustre of the bright lights of London started to be overshadowed by the overcrowding, over-bearing egos and over-priced drinks.

Craig had tried to inject a degree of spontaneity into proceedings after they'd settled back in Edinburgh; a surprise weekend away here and the occasional dinner out with friends. In recent years, however, as their careers accelerated at different speeds, the dirty weekends and raucous dinners had dried up. Their friends began to move away. Or have kids. Or move away and have kids. Or vice versa.

Craig was keen on having some kids of his own. So was Anita. Or so she said. But just as the family planning ventured towards the 'practical' phase, there always seemed to be an impending promotion, series of exams or tetchy argument that cooled Anita's appetite, postponing the prospect of any pittering or pattering.

In recent months, Craig and Anita's peers had started to drop their second sprogs. The stag do's and hen weekends had been replaced with infernal christenings, invariably staged to get little Cameron or Caitlin into that good church school five years hence. Their lives were seemingly on a conveyor belt where they had a limited ability to divert the designated course. And within what seemed like a month, seven years had passed.

Anita was now Operations Director of Corporate Legal. The lofty position came with lots of responsibility, lots of money, long hours and

SUNSET OVER SUNSET © Steve Richards

long absences from Craig, who had stumbled his way through client management jobs at three different marketing agencies into a Sales Manager job that required him to be in London at least two days a week.

Some weeks, Craig wasn't convinced Anita knew he was gone. While away from home, Craig would spend his evenings schmoozing existing clients, prospective clients, lapsed clients and hanging out with existing, prospective and lapsed colleagues.

So, on this particular Wednesday morning, Craig was bored. He was starting to find the whole marketing agency merry-go-round unfulfilling and exhausting. He was up for a career break. If the idea of kids was to be shelved, he wanted six months off to reappraise where he was going and why. At the back of his mind, Craig thought of his father who had worked his proverbial tits off for forty years and never got to enjoy the fruits of his labours, popping his clogs immediately after retirement. He wasn't going to make the same mistake.

This weekend he was going to persuade Anita to ditch the corporate cronies. They were going to rent out the bungalow, sell the car and go on the world tour that had eluded them after graduation. Now, a little older and a lot more financially solvent, they could afford to swap the backpacker hovels for 4-star hotels and take taxis instead of tuc-tucs. The trip would allow them time to reassess their priorities, realign their perspectives and reignite their passion.

This weekend, Craig resolved to float the idea. Run it up Anita's flagpole, so to speak. He'd joke, she'd giggle. Her eyes would light up at the prospect of swapping the daily drudgery for Prosecco in Paris and scuba-diving in the Seychelles. They would shed life's strait-jacket, stick two fingers up at its stealthy suffocation and shoot the breeze in Santiago. They would escape the corporate crusher. At least for a while.

Craig threw his overnight bag into the back of his Vauxhall Corsa with renewed vigour, cheered up by his daydream. Suddenly the prospect of another blurry 48 hours of flight-tune-meeting-schmooze-fawn-sell-meeting-schmoose-repeat-to-fade didn't seem so bad. It might be one of his last trips. The deficit on his sales target suddenly seemed less burdensome. When he was invited into the MD's office the following month for one of his famous 'pep-talks' which tended to be light on

SUNSET OVER SUNSET © Steve Richards

encouragement and heavy on expletive, Craig could retaliate by telling him to stick his smug hubris up his left nostril. Craig was going to take great joy in laying a metaphoric turd in the middle of the rugger bugger's desk by announcing his resignation. If he was feeling particularly punchy on the day itself, he mused at the possibility of laying a real one.

Craig was roused by the last call for his flight. He hurried towards the dwindling queue at the departure gate and, while waiting to step from footbridge onto the plane, he absent-mindedly checked for email. Nothing. Out of habit, he tapped the Facebook icon. He had a friend request from someone called 'Destiny Jones'. His finger hovered above the 'Ignore' button but he rarely got friend requests these days so he tapped through to her profile and realised it was actually from Claire Jones - a friend from Uni days who, for no apparent reason, was now calling herself by the porn-tastic moniker of 'Destiny'. Inspired and excited by the impending new adventures that beckoned in his life, theoretically at least, he decided to grasp the nettle and accept.

After all, what's the worst that could happen..?

3
Destiny Calls

"Get tae fuck," bawled Craig across the table in the basement pub. "See that last burd you were seein', Jimmer, she had a face like her neck'd thrown up!" A burst of laughter and Craig reached for his pint, satisfied he'd repelled the verbal onslaught from one of his old friends.

Craig, Jimmer and a dozen others met once a month to trade insults, sink pints and play poker. The merry band was a mix of old college mates, ex-colleagues and friends of friends. Most of them were considerably better at the insults and the pint-sinking than they were at playing poker. One or two card-sharps, usually the more sober ones, tended to pick up the winnings but for Craig, it was all about letting off some steam and avoiding a lonely hotel room.

"So how's the lovely Anita Craigy-boy?" enquired one of the group of eight, a corpulent cockney called Steve who had been on the same graduate training scheme as Craig and Anita years ago. Steve had spent recent months cultivating a long wispy beard which had become an obvious target for abuse.

"She's battling away, Steve, you know. Keeping the corporate machine running, keeping the economy afloat."

"Beavering away, you say," said Steve, looking across at Jimmer with a wink. "What these women have to do to get ahead in business, eh."

"Giving head, you say," Jimmer interjected. "Is that what you're really trying to say, Stevo?" Craig had shuffled the pack of cards and started dealing them in a wide arc to the players at his table.

"You see, Jimmer," said Craig, "that's always been your problem," he started the second wheel of cards, "fantasising about other people's wives and girlfriends." He set the remaining cards on the table. "You know if you actually put that Xbox down for more than ten seconds and stopped watching online bestiality, you might get yourself a partner one

SUNSET OVER SUNSET © Steve Richards

day." Several boys chortled while perusing their cards. "If you ever had a bath," Craig continued, "you could one day make a blind ugly bloke and his dog really happy."

Jimmer safely put back in his box, Steve asked Craig, "And how is the lovely 'Anita the Maneater'?"

"Big blind, Steve," demanded Craig, reaching to his left across Jimmer to take two blue plastic poker chips from the top of Steve's stack and place them in front of him.

"She pines for you, Steve, obviously." Craig replied, "But somehow she manages to soldier on."

"She's a trooper," said Steve.

"No, seriously, Steve, she misses you," Craig continued, putting two of his own chips into the pot, "like a leper misses a dustpan and brush."

And so the familiar barbs and counter-barbs continued in the tournament of verbal abuse. Insults abounded from around the table, parried and then returned with an extra layer of opprobrium. The battle lines had been drawn for years. Caustic verbal blows were landed, but the mental wounds were always superficial, healed by a concoction of counter-insult and export strength lager.

"So you down on another raiding party from the frozen northern wastelands?" asked Steve as Craig was restacking his chips after a fortuitous win.

"Yeah," Craig replied as another 90s classic drifted from the pub speakers. "Problem is, none of you tight Sassenach bastards are buying." He peered at Steve over his glass and tilted the dregs of his pint into his mouth. "It's a wee bit of a struggle, just now. But it'll pick up. Always does."

Craig stood, threw in his cards then lifted his empty glass towards Steve, adding in a cockney accent, "He who dares, Rodney. He who dares..."

The remainder of the evening progressed customarily. Pints were sunk,

SUNSET OVER SUNSET © Steve Richards

jokes were cracked and Martin, an actuary by trade and semi-pro poker player by volition, pocketed all the cash. Martin was the can opener in the cutlery drawer - he looked a bit like all of the others but he was uniquely equipped to get the job done.

On being summarily despatched from the game in his usual seventh place, Craig shook hands, patted backs, edged his way around the cramped table and said his goodbyes.

"Seeya Jimmer," he said as he slid behind his friend's chair, "Give my regards to the other cons on day-release."

Jimmer replied by extending his middle finger accompanied with a predictably tender riposte.

"Seeya next month, Cuntybollocks. Pass on my regards to all those men in skirts you hang around with up there in Jockoland."

Passing behind Steve's chair, Craig put his hands on his shoulders and squeezed in time with each syllable. "Seeya next month, Gandalf."

Steve's retort was as predictable as it was succinct. "Fuckety off, Numbnuts."

Outside the pub, it was cold and windy. It started to spit. Craig wandered off towards his hotel mulling over several recurring thoughts. Why was he still so shit at poker? Will McDonalds still be open? And why did he never bring a fucking umbrella?

His mood darkened as he traipsed towards the hotel just off Oxford Street. The hotel's interior mirrored Craig's current mood; tired and in need of a woman's touch. He delayed the customary hilarity of a midnight check-in with a clueless hotel receptionist with no grasp of English by taking a detour in search of culinary nirvana: six McNuggets.

Secreting them into his overnight bag to appear slightly less of a sad sap of a salesman, he dug deep to muster a thin smile for the hotel receptionist. Craig tapped on the counter impatiently as the woman tapped on her keyboard. A grimace, then a deep sigh. She looked up slowly at Craig and said, in a clipped Ukrainian accent, "Veery sorrysir,

SUNSET OVER SUNSET © Steve Richards

bud we don have yourrr booking."

Craig gave her his best dead-eyed stare. She continued, "And unforrrtunate, weee arre foolly book tonigh."

Craig's stare plumbed three new depths of dead-eyedness. He then bowed his head, stared resignedly at the scuffed toes of his dog-earred black slip-ons and considered the merits of cyanide capsules.

"Ah, I ha' som goood newss, sirrr" whined the receptionist with the half-smile of a stroke victim. "I get you niiice rome at sisster hotel in Kensing-ton. You jus wait. I call you cab, yesss?"

Craig couldn't summon the energy to get further annoyed. Resigned to his fate and maintaining just enough self-respect to avoid scoffing his congealed chicken supper in front of his Ukrainian nemesis, he stepped into the cool drizzle outside of the hotel entrance. Shoulders drooped, he dropped his overnight bag to the pavement and tried to conjure mental pictures of the Seychelles.

"Craig?" called a female voice out of the surrounding gloom. Slightly startled, Craig scanned the direction of the voice and focussed on the embodiment of sassy allure beaming back at him. 'Craig McGill?" she repeated.

"Er," Craig spluttered.

"I thought it was you," the woman said, tucking a whisp of exquisite brown hair behind her right ear as she quickly bounced towards him.

"Errr," Craig stalled. His eloquence in the face of such beauty defied belief. He was really out of practice.

"I facebooked you this morning and you accepted," cooed the vision of voluptuousness in front of him. Craig's memory jogged as his mind raced.

"Claire! Or, I mean, Destiny..." he said uncertainly. "What are the chances?"

SUNSET OVER SUNSET © Steve Richards

4
Inspector Sands to the Operations Room

Inspector Nick Sands puffed self-consciously on his e-cigarette. He had been badgered to try them by his 11 year-old son when they had met the previous weekend. Nick loved Sam, his son, more than anything on the earth but his boy lived with his wife's family in Forest Hill in south east London, an hour's drive from Nick's flat north of the river.

Sam didn't live with his dad for two reasons. Firstly, Nick's wife, Smita, had died of pancreatic cancer soon after giving birth to their son. Secondly, Nick was an Inspector in the Metropolitan Police.

But these were facts rather than reasons. The facts contributed to the reasons but they were not why father and son lived apart. The real reasons were that firstly, since Smita died Nick had never really had time to bond with his son as he grew up. Smita's extended and very large Indian family had embraced Sam and he seemed happy growing up with his cousins, aunts, uncles and grandparents. Secondly, Nick couldn't cope with being a single parent as well as holding down a relatively senior post in the Met. Something had to give and Nick had regretfully put his job first.

The clincher, however, was that every time Nick looked at Sam, he saw Smita and it broke his heart.

So Nick took another toke of electronically delivered chemicals and pictured Sam's face when he would finally be able to tell his son proudly that he had kicked the cancersticks. The more important priority for Nick Sands, which he acknowledged all too well, was working out how to break the spell of his current reclusive existence, locked away from the world in a silent and lonely flat.

'Inspector Sands' was not the man you might have heard called upon at rail terminals, football grounds and other public events when there's a fire, emergency incident, or, usually, a test of the health and safety procedures. This Inspector Sands wasn't good with crowds. A natural introvert, he liked to hang back and observe rather than blaze any trails. And he was naturally suited to detective work, his observant and perceptive nature unlocking many a criminal conundrum that had befuddled his peers. Since Smita's untimely and tragic demise, Nick had found a new level of invisibility, or 'pigheaded aloofness' as his boss called it. After his wife's death, Nick's extended family had keenly enveloped his son, allowing him to indulge the distraction of throwing himself into his work. His feverish focus had delivered impressive results, and he had jumped up the ranks quickly. He fitted the classic profile of a good detective; no spouse, no live-in dependents, no hobbies. The long hours were a blessing and as the years passed, Nick's reputation grew and the only thing that roused suspicion with the hierarchy was his lack of a drink problem.

A year ago, with Sands in his early thirties, he had been trying to expose a criminal gang that had infiltrated his 'patch'. In central London, there would always be a criminal fraternity, but this particular crew seemed strong on the criminal part but lacking in the fraternity department. They were making money in similar ways to the other gangs - supplying drugs, lending money with exorbitant interest rates - but they had also been linked to a couple of daring smash-and-grab jewellery raids.

Sands noticed that this mob was different. They seemed to be able to achieve a chilling efficiency that was beyond the other criminal brotherhoods. No frills, no fuss, no crowing, these guys were consummate professionals. Whoever was running the operation had an obvious talent for enforcing discipline, not to mention a God-given talent for sadistic torture.

Sands had been studying the gang for a few months with a mixture of horror and admiration. They were extraordinarily secretive and none of the usual informants had anything to say about them. Rumour was they had recruited outside of the local rent-a-thug network. Their targeting - of where, how and with whom to ply their trades - suggested some local knowledge. The only inkling that seemed to recur was a sprinkling of Irish accents.

Sands was aware that many of the paramilitaries from northern and southern Ireland had had their toys taken away by the so-called political peace. 'So-called' because of lot of the racketeering that funded these organisations was still alive and well, even if both sides had stopped the carnage involving civilians, the kind of carnage that gets politicians all twitchy.

In more recent times, the everyday thugs had had to get their kicks, literally, in the Marching Season, or by targeting a particular police station with stones and petrol bombs. The senior delegates had either given up the ghost or diversified into full-time racketeering.

So, a year ago, having tracked developments carefully for months, Sands felt a dart of adrenaline when he got a tip-off from a reliable source that the gang was about to hit a shop on New Bond Street that sold very expensive watches. He had the venue's CCTV upgraded and had adapted its security so the shutters could be brought down by flicking a switch from the road outside, catching the assailants. He had also taken the precaution of placing two experienced officers inside the shop, one posing as a sales assistant, the other a security man. To add one final notch of just-in-case to his belt-and-braces approach, Sands had managed to get sign-off for four additional armed officers at the back of the venue, poised to burst in at an appropriate moment and catch the bad guys red-handed.

So everything was in place and, on the morning of the proposed heist, Sands was satisfied every precaution and preparation had been taken care of. He allowed himself to breakfast at a new, swish coffee shop that had just opened near his house. Shredded wheat wasn't going to cut it, this was going to be a bacon-and-eggs kinda day.

Having just ordered, Sands' phone started to buzz. He stepped outside into the street and during the next 60 seconds, he learned that the plain clothes officer who was to pose as the watch salesman inside the venue that day had just been found dead in a disused garage. He had been strapped to a swivel chair, and one of his arteries had been severed, just under his armpit. He had bled to death seconds before the ambulance crew had reached him. The police had received an anonymous phone call informing them of his whereabouts. When the police arrived, they found their stricken colleague wearing headphones and an iPod in his lap playing a particular track on repeat.

Heart pounding and mind racing, Sands recognised the signature moves of the gang he thought he had out-smarted. Slowly he removed the phone from his ear and took two unsteady steps backwards, staring blankly into space. As he recoiled, someone bumped into him from behind, knocking his left shoulder hard enough for the phone to leave his grasp and go spiralling across the pavement into the gutter. Sands had been knocked off balance and, down on one knee, he instinctively flicked his head left to see a man in a matt black motorbike helmet stride in front of him. Without looking around, the man, in black leather jacket and trousers threw his left leg over a Kawasaki Ninja motorbike and pulled out into the oncoming traffic. In a split second of horror, Sands noticed there was no number plate on the back of the motorbike. In the same second, he felt a warm trickle run down his back. Still on one knee, he reached his left hand round behind him and felt the hilt of a knife. He heard a woman's scream from behind him and he fell forward, face down onto the pavement. Then the world went black.

As Sands thought back to the incident that had changed his life forever, as he had done hundreds of times during his protracted period of recuperation, he reached for his e-cigarette. The thought of these bastards, still going about their business as if nothing had happened, gnawed at his soul. As he drew on the mouth-piece, he wondered if he would ever regain the appetite or the inclination to try to avenge the death of the man who had died on his watch. A man now lay cold in the ground, his remembrance flowers long since wilted, because Sands had somewhere missed a trick.

As he languished in his creaking armchair, Sands pictured his fallen colleague's face. He knew there remained the flicker of a chance he would finally rediscover the courage and conviction to get back to work. But it would not be built on a desire to unmask the man behind his own attempted murder, it would be driven by a deep-seated compulsion – a primordial need - to correct his unknown mistake.

5
Stranger Things

"No, it's fine, er, Destiny, thanks," said Craig unconvincingly, "the looney-toons receptionist has ordered a cab to take me to another hotel. They're overb..."

"Oh, poor you," interrupted Destiny, playfully placing her palms, one at a time, on Craig's shoulders. "Long old day and nowhere to lay this old sleepyhead," she added, ruffling his hair.

Craig looked intently into her eyes. His memory was telling him that Claire Jones was a rather unremarkable girl, with mousy hair, pale complexion and a terrible dress sense. The woman in front of him was definitely the same Claire, but mousy and pale she was not. She presented an all-out assault on Craig's senses, poured into a leather basque-style top to generate a cavernous cleavage, accompanied by dark purple velvet trousers and black knee-length leather boots covered in silver studs.

Her coat was also leather, expensive-looking. Around her delicate, pale neck was a thin black leather strand with large silver cross sitting just above her chest. Her hair was dyed jet-black and was a mass of loose curls, framing her face. Her striking eye makeup and deep purple lipstick completed the picture. In short, she was the sexiest Goth Craig had ever seen. And if Craig wasn't mistaken, she was giving him the signals.

"I haven't seen you for ages, Destiny," said Craig meekly, transfixed by her dark eyes and intoxicated by her alluring, distinctive perfume.

"I know," Destiny agreed. "I was beginning to think you were avoiding me." She giggled. Craig laughed shyly. Behind him, the receptionist appeared.

"Veery sorry, Meester Mac-Jill, but taxi is taking 20 minutes. You come insiiide hotel for warm." She glanced up at the rain now falling steadily from the dark sky before scurrying back inside.

"Looks like you're in a pickle, 'Craig Mac-Jill,'" she mimicked. She

SUNSET OVER SUNSET © Steve Richards

thrust both hands into her jacket pockets and pulled the front of her coat closed. Craig's gaze instinctively dropped 30 centimetres to catch the briefest glimpse of heaving bosom before it disappeared behind the leather gates.

Craig closed his eyes for half a second, desperately trying to regain some semblance of composure.

"Well," he said with a modicum of conviction, making eye contact, "it's a really kind offer, Destiny, it really is, but..."

"Och, tish and pish," Destiny interrupted in a passable Scottish accent, moving in and linking her right arm into Craig's. She started to march them off. Her sudden move towards Craig engulfed him with another powerful waft of musky perfume that took Craig's breath away. He was being swept away, a powerless pawn in her game.

"Do you believe in God, Craig?" she said, swinging her head to meet his gaze as they walked. She was tall in her platform leather boots - only slightly shorter than Craig. Her curls tickled his face as they walked in step.

"God? Er..." Craig said, as they rounded a corner into a side street, the dimmer lighting adding to the feeling of intimate collusion.

She picked up her own thread. "I don't. 'God is a phantom, an apparition created by the rich to sustain and suppress the poor.'" She quickly turned her head again to meet his gaze. "Do you know who said that, Craig?"

He hadn't heard this girl speak his name for well over ten years and now she couldn't stop.

"Alexandre Dumas," she said, throwing her head back as she enunciated the final syllable as 'ass'. "He was a prophet, a poet and wonderfully passionate novelist. If I had a time machine I'd go straight back to meet him. She stopped them both suddenly and again locked her eyes onto his. "Fate is the one true god. Do you ever wish you had a time machine, Craig Mac-Jill?"

"Well..." he said hesitantly. Destiny started walking again, pulling him along.

SUNSET OVER SUNSET © Steve Richards

"Well, well, well," she parroted. "Three wells. That's a lot of water!"

Craig felt like he was falling into a well, deeper and deeper under the spell of this bewitching presence. With his last ounce of self-restraint, it was Craig's turn to bring both of them to an abrupt halt.

"Look, Destiny," he said, turning to stand in front of her, pressing his hands lightly on the sides of her arms. "This is madness. I hear from you out of the blue, after umpteen years, then, boom, you appear like some kind of goddess to rescue me from hotel-overbooking-hell."

"Do you need rescuing, Craig?" she interrupted, turning her head quizzically. "From whom? Or from what?" She was intrigued. "Tell Destiny....ev-er-ything," she said with a theatrical flourish of her left hand which ended with her second and third fingers held horizontally in front of her left eye.

Craig was beginning to think he was on a train bound for the wrong destination. Destiny picked up on his uncertainty.

"Look, Craig," she said, dropping the histrionics. "You need a bed for the night and I happen to live round the corner. It's practical, common sense, that's all." Craig saw Claire Jones appear momentarily from behind the curls and mascara.

"You're right," he said to reassure himself. "Two old friends meeting up by happy coincidence. One helps out the other. Perfectly natural."

"That would be true," she countered, "if coincidence existed. I told you before, Craig," she purred, "there is no such thing as coincidence." She pulled his arm closer more tightly as they walked. "Coincidence and fate are uneasy bedfellows."

They continued to walk eastwards, away from Craig's original lodgings and towards Centrepoint, Oxford Street's eastern bookend, with Marble Arch to the west. After a few seconds, Destiny took a swift right turn and after ten paces she stopped.

"So here we are. Told you it wasn't far."

SUNSET OVER SUNSET © Steve Richards

Craig looked at this temporary abode. It looked impressive - a four-story Edwardian terrace, with ornate brickwork and a large, well-presented black front door adorned by an ornately engraved shiny silver knocker. Destiny unlinked Craig's arm and climbed the five stone steps up to the front door. She paused and looked back down at Craig who was straining his neck, body tilted backwards, trying to see the top of the impressive structure.

"Nice," he said.

"Well, it's central." She remarked. "Now come along, and let's get you out of the cold."

Her tone, confidence and appearance told Craig that Destiny was the type of girl who was used to getting what she wanted. Having come this far, Craig had made his bed and was about to lie in it.

Destiny slammed shut the front door and punched on a light switch that gradually released over time and switched itself off. She had a quick glance at the letters left on the radiator cover, plucked one and then moved to her right to go down some dark stairs.

"Basement flat, I'm afraid." she said over her shoulder. "Not in the penthouse league yet, I'm afraid, darling." She pulled some keys from her leather coat and with a flick of the wrist, the door swung open. She gestured for him to enter first then followed him inside and shut the door.

The first thing that struck him was the aroma; the air was heavy and infused with a strong smell of incense. It wasn't unpleasant but it was strong. The light that Destiny had flicked on was pale green which bathed the flat's corridor in a dull, verdant glow. As she walked in front of Craig, Destiny's silhouette was picked out by a slightly brighter light in the room to where she was headed, towards the back of the flat. On entering what appeared to be her lounge, Craig stopped, dropped his overnight bag to the floor and look around. What met his eyes was a scene from a Turkish hookah lounge. To his left, a floor-to-ceiling bookcase stretched the full width of the room, choked with hundreds of leather-bound tomes. In front, an L-shaped sofa in leopard-print stretched out, only a few centimetres off the floor, covered in a huge, ornate purple rug, the kind you'd expect to find in Istanbul's Grand Bazaar.

SUNSET OVER SUNSET © Steve Richards

An old-fashioned standard lamp provided the light, tinged with a yellow glow as the bulb was enveloped by a mustard-coloured velvet lampshade. In front of the sofa was a coffee table, littered with various glossy magazines and, strikingly, a huge photography book. From its front cover, a blindfolded naked woman, pictured in black and white, sat on a child's wooden rocking horse. Her eyes were covered with a black leather blindfold and she looked like she would have been screaming had it not been for the tennis ball shoved into her mouth. Both her nipples were pierced with silvery bolts. Craig was transfixed by the image as Destiny returned from the furthest room in the flat, the kitchen.

"I know," she said, following his gaze. "Delicious image, isn't it."

Craig remained spell-bound. The girl looked familiar.

"My boss paid for the shoot," she continued. "All I had to do was get my bangers out."

It dawned on Craig that his hostess was astride the horse in the picture.

"Mmm," he mustered. "Striking."

"Look, darling," Destiny said, taking Craig's chin and turning his head to meet his gaze. "You make yourself at home. I need to go and close up the bar at the club. Won't be long." She leant in and kissed Craig's forehead then immediately reached up and rubbed out the mark left by her lipstick.

"Wh..." Craig spluttered.

"Will only be an hour, my sweet." She was already walking back along the hallway towards the front door. "I think there's a bottle of ouzo in the fridge. Help yourself. Two hours tops. Front bedroom is the spare one, darling." She stopped and turned to face him. "Or we can top and tail!" she let out a squawking laugh and disappeared.

SUNSET OVER SUNSET © Steve Richards

6
Electrifying Presence

"So what you're really saying, Donald, is 'Seamus, you're a thick, short-arsed Irish cunt.'"

Donald sat, ashen-faced, opposite Seamus in his office in a backroom of The Sunset burlesque club near Holborn in central London. It was after midnight on a Wednesday night, the time when Seamus cut deals, made plans and, on this occasion, intimidated his rival.

"It's not like tha...." said Donald, a thick-set Londoner in his early thirties, the son and right-hand man of one of the gangland bosses who had been around for decades. Seamus's operation had encroached on their turf. They had undercut his prices of illegal narcotics. And they were supplying a better product. Their supply line was also more consistent, so Donny Blanchard, the man at the head of affairs, had had enough. He had sent his eldest son, Donald, heir to his business empire, to tell this Irish invader to back off, or face some unpalatable consequences.

Donny was a firm believer in keeping things simple so a forthright conversation in the first instance, followed by some mindless violence, if necessary, was the process that had delivered results over the years. But this Irish crew, bossed by Seamus Twite, was relentless. They were professional, well organised and, well, relentless. So it was time to draw a firm line in the sand, or Donny & Son's days seemed numbered.

"If it's not like that," said Seamus, finishing Donald's sentence for him, his cheeks darkening. "But that's what it sounds like from this side of the desk."

The desk in question was huge, two metres long and at least a metre wide, its dark mahogany frame topped with a dark green leather rectangle that extended to within 10cms of each side. The leather was embossed with an elaborate pattern of gold swirls. The desk mirrored its owner; it meant business, it was hard as nails, and it wasn't going anywhere.

SUNSET OVER SUNSET © Steve Richards

Donald, leaning back in the wooden chair sat opposite Seamus, was desperately trying to look relaxed. It's a difficult act to pull off, especially when his stomach felt like it was tied in a knot that was being twisted. He looked around himself - a preferable view to meeting the Irishman's piercing dark eyes that never seemed to blink. Donald saw a wood-panelled room with no windows, no pictures and very few decorative accoutrements.

The den's most notable feature was a glass case mounted on the wall to Seamus's left. Inside the sturdy box, fastened to a dark green baize base, was a row of eight hunting knives. Each had a 20cm blade in a slightly different shape. One that caught Donald's eye had a sleek smooth curve on one length of the blade, with a series of patterned serrations on the other. The gleaming steel picked out the shape of the unfurled wing of a small bird, sweeping inwards to meet the hilt which looked like it was made of marble, or ivory. The threat the knives presented was minimal in Donald's estimation. They looked like a decorative feature, the kind you might see in a war museum, used by warriors from another epoch. But well lit, the blades of perfectly precise steel reflected the glow of the desk lamps that balanced each side of the desk.

"Now you listen to me, Donald," Seamus said menacingly, leaning forward to rest both elbows on his desk, lowering his forearms towards his guest. "I might be Irish, but I'm no cunt. And I've seen some cunts in my time, Donald, let that be clear. Do you understand me?"

Donald stared back at him, trying his best to show no sign of weakness. A twitch at the corner of the left hand side of his mouth, however, gave Seamus the tell-tale signal that his approach was having its desired effect. Seamus warmed to his task.

"So if I'm a cunt, Donald, and you're a prick, the only reason you're here, here in MY office, in MY club, is because you want to fuck me."

Donald shifted slightly in his seat, glancing down at his shoe, a wry smile starting to crack.

"So do you want to fuck me, Donald? Pricks fuck cunts. I learned that in medical school."

SUNSET OVER SUNSET © Steve Richards

Donald knew he had to get his next sentence right. He opened his mouth to speak then closed it, stealing a few more seconds to make sure he chose the right words.

"Ok, Seamus, you've had your say so let me have mine," said Donald, his voice steady and confident. "Firstly, let me assure you, I'm not here to engage in any sort of sexual practice."

Seamus leaned back in his chair, touching the fingertips on both hands together lightly, a wry grin on his lips.

"Secondly," added Donald, "I'm here to pass on a message from my old man, Donny, who I think you might be aware of."

Seamus sat in his chair across the desk. He had fixed his quarry with his fiercest glare. He was now not moving a single muscle while he listened. His smile had subsided. Conversely, Donald's body language was twitchy and a bead of sweat had appeared just below his hairline.

He continued, "The message is simple: back off."

Seamus sat perfectly still, gaze fixed.

"You need to understand that enough is enough," insisted Donald. "You've been treading on our toes now for at least two years."

Seamus's cheeks started to flush. He was statuesque. Donald's confidence was starting to waver under the stare of his implacable foe. He looked straight into Seamus's eyes.

"It needs to stop."

Donald's eyes flitted to his right and poised for a split second on the contents of the glass cabinet on the wall.

"And it needs to stop, er, now," Donald's voice tailed off. The final word was barely a whisper.

"That it?" snapped Seamus, his tone, volume and accent combining to regain eye-contact with Donald instantaneously.

"That the full extent of daddy's message?" He spat the last word as a verbal bullet.

"You come into my club to try to warn me off. You sit in my office and expect me to curtail my business interests because daddy's feeling the squeeze? Have you half-wits not heard of market forces? Well, I too have a message, Donald-me-lad, which I intend to deliver personally."

Donald started to inspect his shoes again. Seamus's voice dropped an octave and ten decibels.

"Look at me, Donald."

Donald brushed an imaginary piece of fluff from the lap of his jeans.

"LOOK AT ME!" Seamus bellowed, his words exploding across the desk. Donald's eyes snapped back. One bead of perspiration had become eight. Seamus leaned forward and placed both sets of fingers on the desk, his thumbs under the ledge of the desktop.

Seamus continued. "Now I'm going to continue to take candy from your dad's baby. In fact, I'm going to redouble my efforts, step up my operation and specifically target your interests. Be under no illusion that coming here was a mistake, Donald,"

Seamus started to stand slowly and Donald instinctively started to follow suit.

"SIT THE FUCK DOWN!" Seamus shouted. Donald slumped back in his seat and at the exact second his backside hit the seat Seamus depressed the button under his desk with his left thumb. Donald let out a yelp and sprung back to his feet. He had received a strong and painful electric shock. Behind him, two large men had silently entered the room and now stood behind Donald's chair, one either side.

"I thought I'd told you to sit down," said Seamus, standing opposite his prey, leaning forward on both straightened arms which anchored his pose on the desktop. Donald glanced at Seamus's hands. Both thumbs were still obscured. Donald then sensed someone behind him and noticed the two musclemen for the first time. He physically flinched

SUNSET OVER SUNSET © Steve Richards

and his last ounce of composure deserted him.

"Don't make me ask you again, Donald," Seamus said with a slight shake of the head. Donald stared down at the chair. He too started to shake his head.

"Now you look here, Seamus...." Donald's eyes flitted from bouncers, to their rubber-soled shoes, to the chair, then back to Seamus. "My dad..."

Seamus gave an almost imperceptible nod towards his henchmen and in unison they reached forward to put one hand on each of Donald's shoulders, pulling him back so he regained his seat.

"But, Donald, daddy's not here," said Seamus lifting his right arm to wave it around the office to illustrate his point. He now had his victim just where he wanted him and the sound-proofing of the entire venue, insisted upon at great expense by the council in the interests of local residents, was going to come in useful. He replanted his arm on the desk and pushed the button. Donald emitted a high-pitched scream as his body contorted in an agonised spasm. He tried to jump up but was prevented by two huge tree-trunk-thick tattooed arms, one leaning heavily on each shoulder.

Donald stared back desperately at Seamus's granite-like features. Tears stared to well in the corners of both eyes. He then closed them and was made to scream some more.

SUNSET OVER SUNSET © Steve Richards

7
Stab in the Dark

His wife's sudden bereavement had taken its toll on Nick Sands. He had ploughed his focus into his job and when that upward move was derailed by the motorcyclist's knife, his soul-searching began. After some 'why me?' angst, realisation became frustration which then turned into anger. Sands recognised all the signs and moved into his acceptance phase with an air of bleak resignation. His resources had been sapped. His vitality levels were negligible. As his brother-in-law put it succinctly, 'his lust for life had fully fucked off.'

His dead wife's family had tried everything to defibrillate his joie de vivre. They had taken over full responsibility for Sam, his son, who was doing remarkably well considering he had lost both parents, one mortally and the other emotionally.

The assassin's knife should really have killed him. It missed his major organs and arteries by millimetres and his recovery, physically at least, had only taken two months. Since then, the dutiful visits from colleagues had dried up and Sands had taken introversion to a new level. Some weeks he didn't leave the house at all. Smita's brother, Anil, being of similar age, had been given the task of shaking his brother-in-law out of his malaise. Earlier that same Wednesday, Anil decided it was time to try to prize a man out of social hibernation.

"You look well," Anil lied through the crack in the opened door. Sands had ignored the first three rings of the doorbell. This tactic got rid of the vast majority of passing tradesmen, the odd local politician and even the Jehovah's Witnesses. On the fourth ring, Sands knew the face he would see smiling at him from his doorway.

Anil was a lovely guy. The consummate family man, he shared the large house with his parents, wife and two kids, sister and her husband and her younger child. And Sam Sands.

Anil had kept his ace - bringing Sam to see his dad - up his sleeve. His first objective was to try to prize Sands out of his house and try to get him going again; to jump-start this man's life and get at least a flicker of light behind his eyes before he brought his son round to see him. A visit from his son might, of course, supply the spark but Anil didn't want to risk him seeing his dad in his current state of torpor.

Sands had his foot wedged behind the front door and spoke to Anil though the narrow crack. "Look, Anil, I know you've the best of intentions..."

"Bit more colour in your cheeks," interrupted Anil. "Not as much as me, mind, but you're looking less like a sight-screen at Lord's." The cricket reference was carefully selected by Anil as he planned what he was going to say on the drive over.

"Ah, that reminds me," he teased. "Guess who has two tickets to England versus India this Sunday?" He produced two tickets from behind his back and flourished them in between their faces.

The crack in the door began to close. Anil was expecting it and jammed his own boot into the remaining gap. It reopened slightly. Anil noticed a least a week's stubble on Sands' chin. He looked terrible, with a huge dark circle under each eye. Anil increased the urgency.

"Nick, man, come on, it's me. You don't answer your phone or texts. What am I supposed to do? You know what the family's like. You gotta give me something to report back."

Sands stared at him with deadpan eyes. Anil continued.

"Look, them tickets weren't cheap you know. I had to go back on the game. And you know the grief I get from Rupinda when I unleash the trunk of funk for money." Anil embellished the last few words by grabbing his own crotch and thrusting his hips forward. He followed it up with the broadest smile he could summon in the face of such apathy.

The door swung shut and Anil watched through the patterned glass as the shape of his brother-in-law's back walked away from him down the hallway.

Anil called at the door, "Come on, man! Work with me on this, Nick." He

SUNSET OVER SUNSET © Steve Richards

banged his fist three times in quick succession on the glass to signal his frustration. "You can't shut yourself away forever. Sam needs his dad!" Anil pushed his nose onto the glass to get a better view and thought he noticed the blurred shape of Sands' back pause at his final plea. It stayed still for three full seconds before shuffling off and disappearing into the gloom.

8
Ouzo Sorry Now?

Craig sank, low, very low, onto Destiny's sofa. He had been mildly startled at her sudden disappearing act and he found himself alone in a strange flat. He glanced at his watch: past midnight. The inner glow caused by the pints consumed earlier at poker night was starting to recede.

He considered his options. The sensible choice, of course, was to leave a polite note, retrace his steps to the hotel and get in the cab to the sister hotel. No harm done. The second option was to get a glass of water, retreat to the spare bedroom, set his alarm for an early start and skedaddle first thing in the morning. No harm done either.

Craig clambered back to his feet and started to wander slowly towards the brighter light coming from the kitchen. The third option, he pondered, was not sensible. It did not involve water, retreating or the faintest hint of a skedaddle.

He opened the fridge. 'Sparsely populated' barely did it justice. Inside, a bottle of ouzo and a bottle of tequila sat in the compartment in the fridge door and two and a half lemons sat alone on the shelves of the fridge interior. The half-lemon was showing signs of decay and Craig estimated it was spliced asunder at least two days ago.

Craig had always hated tequila, his opinion forever stained by a night out almost twenty years earlier that had ended with him waking up sat in a bath of cold water, fully clothed. On opening his eyes, his body's involuntary reaction to his predicament was to deposit the contents of his stomach and bowels, with violent force from both ends, into the cold water. Craig had exited the bathroom shivering uncontrollably and he had walked home covered in chunks of his own puke and worse. An enduring mental note was made and since then, even the smell of tequila made Craig twitch.

The bottle of ouzo twinkled in the light of the fridge. Craig reached down and he resolved to delay making a decision on his options while he

SUNSET OVER SUNSET © Steve Richards

sipped at a large measure of Greek firewater. The taste was awful but the fact it was cold took the sour edge off and Craig could feel the warming effect of the alcohol begin to reignite his sense of adventure.

Leaving the kitchen, he scanned the lounge from a different perspective and the first thing he noticed was that there was no TV. The bookcase covering one wall was mirrored by a small fireplace and narrow hearth. On the mantelpiece sat a row of a dozen small mystical trinkets of various shapes, sizes and colours. Intrigued, Craig started at the one nearest him and perused a series of candle-holding glass cups, intricately carved miniature wooden animals and ornately patterned silver curiosities. The room had the feel of either a louche speakeasy or crack den. Craig hadn't yet worked out which.

His taste buds increasingly desensitised to the acrid taste of his drink, Craig wandered back down the hall towards the front door. The door to the first room on his right was shut. Suddenly a wave of anxiousness shivered down Craig's spine. What if someone else was in the flat? Destiny hadn't expressly said they were on their own. Did the closed door in front of him mean someone was asleep inside?

He shuffled past the door and pressed on towards two more interior doors further along the corridor. Both were ajar.

On peering round the first door, he found a small bathroom with a shower cubicle in one corner. His right elbow lightly brushed the wallpaper as he moved along the cramped space, the feeling of claustrophobia heightened by the dark swirls on both walls and dingy lighting. He reached the second doorway and peered in. He listened intently and, taking the largest swig yet of his drink, he nudged the door open with the end of his right shoe.

The resistance was reasonably strong and Craig noticed a thick brown carpet impeding its progress. He transferred his glass from his right to left hand and, leaning his shoulder on the door frame, he reached across the doorway, slid his right hand into the darkness of the interior wall and felt around for a light switch. He found it and flicked it on.

Nothing happened.

He tried the switch again, twice, but the dimness prevailed. Now standing opposite the door, cupping his ouzo in both hands, he leaned slightly back and sent his right leg forwards to lever the door open another few centimetres. He peered in and saw a black silhouette on the far wall of the room staring straight at him. It was completely motionless. Craig's heart immediately began to pound harder in his chest. He stood for a second, mimicking the immobility of the brooding shape. Between him and the dark outline, Craig noticed a small double bed, neatly made, covered by a lavishly decorated batik-style throw, fringed all around the edge by golden tassels. His eyes flicked back towards the silhouette and in the few seconds that had passed, Craig's eyes had become accustomed to the darkness just enough to notice a further detail about the shape that stared back. It appeared to have a head shaped more like a large cat than a human.

He edged forwards, crossing the boundary from hallway into room and noticed a lamp on the bedside table nearest him. Staring intently at the dark shape he moved slowly to his left, leaned downwards, reached forward and upwards to feel for a switch within the upturned bowl of the lampshade.

Craig then felt something brush his right leg and he froze. He glanced down but saw nothing. He found the switch and pushed it away from him. The room was suddenly bathed in a dim light. Craig glanced towards his foot and then instantaneously over at the shape on the wall. Straightening his legs slowly to regain his full height he noticed that his would-be assailant was a black statue, matching his eye-line. Made of jet-black porcelain, the figure possessed the featureless head of Siamese cat. The shape's human shoulders supported two arms that reached down to hold the hilt of a sword which stretched down in between the shape's human legs. The sword's point disappeared into the thick carpet in between two feet.

Craig then glanced back up to the figure's torso which featured two human-style naked breasts. He felt his shoulders relax slightly and then felt something else brush past the calf of his leg. He glanced down and saw a jet black cat. This one, however, was real and it stared up a Craig from a sitting position.

He sat on the bed with his back to the huge cat-faced sword-holder

SUNSET OVER SUNSET © Steve Richards

and put his glass on the bedside table. He looked around then, out of the corner of his eye, he saw something else move and his instinctively twitched his neck to look upwards. He then realised that the whole ceiling area, right up to each edge of the room, was covered by a huge mirror. He looked at himself taking another sip of his drink and raised both eyebrows.

"Fuck. In. Hell, Craigy-boy. What the fuck are you doing here?" he mumbled to himself.

After sitting there for a minute or two, Craig left the bedroom, walked back past the bathroom and then slowed down as he passed the shut door. There was a faint light escaping from underneath. As he crept past, he leaned his left ear closer, listening for any faint noise that might provide a clue as to its occupancy. Craig was interrupted by another push against his leg - the cat obviously liked him and was looking for some company.

From a young age, Craig had never really developed much of an affinity with felines. Unlike any other pets, the balance of power with cats was different; more equal. They weren't dependent on their owners and in Craig's experience seemed to strut around their homes with an independent arrogance. The black specimen spooking Craig fell into that category - it wanted some attention and Craig felt obliged to comply. He shooed the cat gently along the hallway with gentle help from his right shoe.

Back in the lounge, Craig wondered why he was being so timid. Time for some more ouzo. Just a wee nip, he thought, to inject some relaxation and confidence into proceedings. He returned from the kitchen with renewed resolve and his eye was drawn to one section of the bookcase that contained stacked vinyl LPs instead of books. He looked around and spotted a small record player hiding under one corner of the low-slung sofa.

He flicked through the record collection: mainly obscure jazz and world music. Some really obscure stuff Craig had never heard of. Some Turkish recordings from the 70s, a group called 'Jon K' called Kings of Calypso, with a particularly dog-eared record sleeve. He then discovered something more familiar: an album from the mid-90s that Craig had on

CD called 'K' by Kula Shaker. It was largely guitar-based indie music that Craig liked, but heavily infused with Indian overtones; lots of sitars and a liberal sprinkling of Hindu chanting. Different.

Craig freed the record player, plugged it in, opened the top and tipped the sleeve to reveal the vinyl. He hadn't played a vinyl record for two decades or more. He put the needle in the groove and sat back onto the sofa to hear the faint wail of pipes and drums build. The ouzo was starting to kick in now and Craig felt a wave of tiredness wash over him. He pulled out his iPhone and checked his diary for the next day. Nothing until 10.30am. Nice relaxed start. He set the alarm for 8.30am and stuffed the rectangle back into his jeans. The cat jumped up onto the sofa.

"Alright, catkins," Craig said out loud. He reached out his left arm towards his furry companion. The cat sniffed at the tips of his fingers suspiciously.

"Kula Shaker, ouzo and hot black pussy," he said out loud. "Sometimes you never know what's round the corner, eh."

He took another sip and wondered at the improbable coincidence of getting the friend request on Facebook then 'bumping into' someone who he hadn't seen for years on the same day. Million-to-one shot. It triggered another tingle of uneasiness in the pit of his stomach which he immediately extinguished with another large swallow of the clear liquid in his glass. He slumped his head backwards to rest on the back of the sofa and hummed along to the music.

9
'Into the Deep'

Fearful of succumbing to slumber, Craig thrust his head forward and the huge book on the coffee table again caught his eye. He flicked through to reveal a succession of mainly black and white photos of people trussed up in various instances of leather. Self-consciously, he turned the pages with a mix of excitement, self-loathing and intrigue. Destiny appeared repeatedly throughout the book. In the variety of poses, she looked fierce, confident and completely captivating. The pictures were well-produced, expensively shot. Men and women were captured in various states of pain or ecstasy, or both. The images were steamy but not pornographic.

The most striking image was the one featuring Destiny sat astride on a child's rocking horse. She had a whip in her hand and a tall black man with long dreadlocks was on all fours in front of her. His eyes were closed and he had thrown his head back. He looked like he was killing himself laughing.

Craig glanced down and noticed that he had euphemistically pitched a tent in his trousers. He rolled his eyes and slapped the book shut. He started to feel that he should sound the retreat and seek the solace of the spare room duvet overseen by the po-faced porcelain puss.

By way of a compromise, he crept back along the corridor, eyeing the lamplight protruding from under the first bedroom suspiciously. On reaching the bathroom, and physically unable to alleviate the pressure on his bladder because of his enduring erection, he thought the best bet might be to 'unleash the hounds'. He fumbled inside his trousers for a few seconds and then his heart jumped at the sound of the front door slamming shut.

"Craig!" came the call from the corridor followed by quick footsteps. "Did you wait up, dahling?"

Craig removed his hands from his boxer shorts and put them either side of the sink. He stared at himself for a second in the mirror and then bowed his head and closed his eyes. By this time his hostess had already bounded along into the lounge, not seen her guest and had started to retrace her steps along the corridor.

Craig was pulling his trousers up when a playful knock on the door coincided with the lilting enquiry, "Are you in there, Craig?"

Destiny was obviously in high spirits and was singing her sentences through the wooden panel that separated her from her audience.

"Come out, come out, whoever you are!"

Craig opened the door and tried his best to act cool. Some people could pull off an air of suave nonchalance in stressful situations. Craig wasn't one of them.

On noticing his hint of fluster, Destiny stared at him, holding her cat in her arms, and declared, "Ooh, Craig. You look slightly queasy, dahling. Like you've been downing ouzo, stroking my pussy then having a wank." She erupted in a fit of giggles.

Craig stared at her, unable to respond for all of a second and then spluttered, "Ha! Oh, er. Yeah. Er, I mean, no! Just a call of nature, you know..."

He filed back along the corridor towards the lounge and Destiny followed him close behind, playfully pushing him along in front of her.

"Now, you go back in there and fix us both a little dinky-poos and I'll get changed and we can have a proper catch up."

The final words drifted off as she opened and closed the previously shut door to the second bedroom. Craig glanced back over his left shoulder to see her waltzing into the room, ripping open her bodice as she flounced. The other thing he noticed via his brief glimpse into the vixen's boudoir was that it was decorated like a Bedouin's harem and appeared to be otherwise unoccupied. He had been unnecessarily reticent. The final thing he noticed as the door swung shut was a pair of silver handcuffs dangling from the headboard.

SUNSET OVER SUNSET © Steve Richards

Craig's forward propulsion landed him back in the lounge. He paused for a second then regained just enough composure to pick up his glass en route to the kitchen. The brighter lighting seemed to stimulate his wits and he purposefully set about pouring two drinks.

When he returned into the lounge, Destiny was perched on the low-slung couch with her back to him. She had retrieved the album cover from the floor and was inspecting it.

"Underrated, this album," she said as he walked around behind her, posting her drink over her left shoulder. As his hand touched her t-shirt, her hand automatically moved up to clutch the glass.

"And I see someone has been looking at my saucy pictures," she said with playful admonishment, nodding towards the photography book.

"Yes," said Craig. "Quite revealing."

He glanced at Destiny who was now sporting a light grey cotton crop-top, white knee-length socks and black knickers. Craig noticed there was no hint of a bra under the t-shirt. He instinctively averted his gaze. He knew Destiny was noticing every flinch.

Kula Shaker's lead singer, Crispian Mills finished another one of his trademark caterwauls accompanied by a crescendo of sitars and drums as Destiny spoke.

"I always wanted to do a proper shoot. My boss at The Sunset club, where I work, paid for the lot."

She studied the look on Craig's face.

"No!" she reached over and touched his nose with her index finger. "It's not *that* kind of club, Craig.' She sipped her drink.

"It's a burlesque club. Dancing girls. Singers. The odd novelty act. We had a dog that played the harmonica last week. It's not a seedy la-la-bar. We serve sushi for God's sake!"

He tried to fix his best dead-pan expression but then lifted one eyebrow.

"Ok, Sherlock, I know that look. Yes, I used to dance. I used to flaunt it." She jiggled her chest. "Hey, if you're gonna be like that," she held out both wrists towards him, "put the cuffs on now, Officer, and take me Downtown."

Craig's mind flitted back to the cuffs he'd seen by her bed.

Destiny drained her drink, then leaned back. "Anyway," she said, "Enough about lil' 'ole me. What have you been up to all these years?"

Craig was still fighting the mental picture of the handcuffs and the possible nuances of what Destiny meant by 'taking her Downtown' when he realised he'd been invited to take an active role in the conversation.

"Well," he began, "you know. Working a lot."

He glanced across at Destiny who had repositioned herself on the couch so she was sitting cross-legged, directly facing him. She scratched the side of her left breast absent-mindedly.

"I got married," he continued, "to Anita. Not sure if you remember her fro..."

"'Anita the Maneater!'" Destiny shrieked. "Oh, Craig, she was a MINX!"

Unsure whether she was taking the piss, Craig pushed on.

"Yeah, well, she is, working really hard too. She is doing really well too." He felt self-conscious under Destiny's unblinking stare. "She is..."

"'She' this, 'her'' that," Destiny interrupted again. "Anita's not here, Craig. It's you I want to hear about. Where have you BEEN all my life," she threw her head back after the final few words and let out another cackle of laughter.

Craig took another sip and started to wish he'd waited for that cab.

SUNSET OVER SUNSET © Steve Richards

10
Who's the Daddy?

"I don't give a cunting fuck who you think you are, Irish," came the voice down the phone as Seamus sat back in his office chair, a sly smile seeping to the corners of his mouth. He had been waiting in his office until late as he was looking forward to catching up with Donald's dad, Donny.

"I'm gonna take great pride in chopping you up, meself." Donny's cockney brogue rasped down the phone as Seamus mulled over when to engage the Neanderthal in conversation. Not quite yet.

"You elecrify my facking first-born. I mean what sort of sick Irish midget cant electrifies people?"

Donny's rage was gathering momentum.

"And the facking nerve! I hope you've made a facking will, Irish, plain I do. This is no idle threat. I'm gonna end you Irish. Proper."

A pause.

"You still facking there....?"

"Electrocute," Seamus said into the receiver in a low, controlled and unemotional voice.

"You what?" said Donny. "You facking what?"

Seamus imagined the small pieces of foam emanating from Donny's mouth in his usual bar in Catford, south-east London.

"Electrocute," Seamus repeated. "It's 'electrocute', not 'electrify'," he said casually. "So many Englishmen and yet so few who can speak the Queen's English."

"You're taking the facking piss, Irish. I'm calling you personally. Me, taking time and trouble to call you meself and I get fun and facking games. Well, in all my..."

Seamus smiled again, then silently mouthed to himself a countdown from three, two, one, then shot the receiver away from his ear as Donny exploded in rage at the other end of the line.

"You facking bog-trotting Fenian cant, you. Facking potato muncher! Talking to me like I'm a facking no-mark. All my facking days, I..."

"Leprechaun," said Seamus sharply interrupting.

"'Leprechaun'?" Donny instinctively repeated.

"You missed out, 'leprechaun' from your list of cartoon anti-Irish insults. 'Fenian, potato-munching leprechaun cant'" taunted Seamus. "Let's make sure we get the full lexicon of hackneyed, bigoted jibes out of your system, Donny. Why not? Feel better now? Got it off your chest, old timer?"

"I'm not listening to this facking..." Donny said in disbelief.

Seamus moved quickly in his seat to lean forward, deadly serious.

"Then listen to this, Donny." His tone had changed, any hint of mirth gone. He pulled the receiver close to his mouth, his features suddenly twisted in violent and vindictive aggression.

"I'm fed up with you and your sad-sap-of-a-son. I'm sick of your threats. I'm tired of your old-school posturing and I want you to get one thing into your ill-educated skull. My organisation and I are going *nowhere*. We will continue to operate as we see fit. Market forces. Supply and demand. Our product is better produced, better supplied and better marketed. If you have one last modicum of common sense, you will realise you're out of your depth here, Donny. You can't win this fight. Go back to your scrap yards, your car rings and your skip hire businesses because if you persist on your current track, things are going to end very quickly and very messily for you, your family and your extended family. This is a lecture I only ever give once. You'd be wise to act on it."

SUNSET OVER SUNSET © Steve Richards

He calmly replaced the receiver into the old-fashioned cradle. Seamus picked up his crystal tumbler of neat Jamieson's whiskey, put the liquid to his lips, paused then took a sip. He knew that approximately 12 miles away, a large cockney would be screaming like a banshee.

SUNSET OVER SUNSET © Steve Richards

11
Sands of Time

The loud trill of the phone cut through the silence in Nick Sands' flat. The noise shattered the silence and made him physically jump. He had just eaten some lunch and dozed off in his armchair then this rude interruption clattered into his world.

Nick had considered disconnecting the phone-line. But then he had worried about his son not being able to reach him. He had caller ID but his current caller wasn't recognised so he let it ring. It seemed to be getting louder the more it rang. Nick closed his eyes to steel himself against the din.

It would stop soon. Even those energy supplier sales calls gave up after ten unanswered rings. But this caller was persistent. A sixth sense told Nick this was not a sales call. He put his hand on top of the receiver and let it ring four more times, eyes still closed. Anything to stop the infernal noise. Make it stop.

"Hello," Sands croaked, his voice barely audible. He hadn't uttered a word out loud for three days since the Tesco delivery man had arrived to provide some basic sustenance.

"Inspector?" came the reply in a surprised voice. "In-, er, is that Inspector Sands?" stammered the caller. "Is that you?"

"It would seem so," Sands deadpanned.

"I've got someone who wants to speak to you, Inspector."

Sands heard some muffled chat in the background. There was an urgency that contrasted sharply with the catatonic stillness pervading his lounge.

A crackle. Ruffled papers. A familiar voice just away from the receiver said, "Ok, thanks, Dave…"

SUNSET OVER SUNSET © Steve Richards

"Nick!" John Randwick boomed down the line. "Thought you'd gone into permanent hibernation."

"That was the plan," Sands mono-toned.

"Right, well," Randwick continued. "It's time to catch a grip 'cos I need you."

There it was. The sentence Nick Sands had been dreading.

"You still there, Nick..?"

"Yep. I'm here." Sands' voice was a disembodied whisper.

"Look, Nick. You know me. I wouldn't call if it wasn't important. Well this isn't just important, it's necessary. Nick, are you listening...?"

Detective Sergeant John Randwick's tone had evolved from sympathetic to grateful to business-like and now impatience.

"Yes, alright, John. I'm listening. What is it?"

Randwick had been instrumental in pushing Nick Sands' promotion to Inspector. A thick-set bearded man in his early 50s, Randwick's nose for solving crime extended to spotting investigative talent as well as excellent Italian red wine. He had seen many come and go but he had spotted a quiet, assured confidence in Sands and when the opportunity to arose, several other noisier candidates seemed ahead of Nick. But a word in the right direction from Randwick – combined with three impressive interviews – and Sands had got the job.

He then spent several years proving Randwick right. He had the unteachable knack for seeing the invisible connections that linked crimes to their perpetrators. While police training was increasingly good at showing people where, how and what to look for, for some people the dots seemed to join more quickly and instinctively.

Randwick and Sands had formed a solid partnership and the whole department's reputation was on the up. But Sands' stabbing a year or so ago was robbing Soho CID of its quietest, most unassuming and

SUNSET OVER SUNSET © Steve Richards

stringently potent weapons.

In recent months, the performance stats had started to decline and John Randwick had been entrusted to persuade the team's best player back into the game.

"Look," said Randwick, "when I took that bullet 20 years ago, it shook me badly. My old dear mum wanted me to hang up my truncheon. But I knew I was cut out to be a Copper. I wasn't any good at anything else and I loved the chase. I see that in you, Nick."

"I've been expecting you to call, John," came the reply. Randwick's charm offensive was being drowned out by a wave of apathy.

"Then you must realise that we need you back," Randwick countered. "Doesn't that mean anything, Nick? Come on, man, speak to me, Nick!" he implored.

He was not about to beg. He didn't do begging. Randwick sensed that his colleagues in the department that Wednesday evening had all stopped what they were doing to eavesdrop his conversation. They all wanted him back too. Randwick looked around and scowled at them, waving his arm in a circle to shake them back into action.

"I'm done, John," said Sands in a firm voice. "I don't need it any more. Sam needs me more than you do. It's not fair on him. He can't lose two parents. It would destroy him."

Randwick changed tack. "Righto, Nick. Chuck it in. I think you can stay on the sick for another four months. They might pension you off after that, but you'll need to get a job. Security man at one of those hotels. Or a government building. Minimum wage. Night shifts. Twenty five years - which will seem like fifty - of regretting one decision."

Randwick now injected some sympathy into his tone for the first time as he continued. "And what's Sam going to think of his dad then? The dad he never sees. The dad who used to be the hero policeman who then sits behind a reception desk bored off his nut. The dad who's skint, alone and miserable all the time."

SUNSET OVER SUNSET © Steve Richards

Randwick paused, wondering if he had gone in too hard or whether he should add one more layer. Silence at the other end of the line. He softened his tone further and added. "For Sam's sake, Nick. That's exactly why you should come back."

Randwick listened intently. He feared the line had gone dead and that his plea had gone unheard. More silence. Then a quiet voice spoke.

"You're a bastard, John." Several more seconds passed. "Call me back tomorrow morning and tell me all about it."

12
The Mangle

Craig awoke to a searing pain behind his eyes. He closed them immediately and came to a one-word conclusion.

Ouzo.

On reopening, he glanced to his left to find the 6ft black porcelain cat seemingly looking down on him judgmentally.

"You can fuck off," Craig said, under his breath.

His mouth felt like he'd been gargling a sawdust and bleach cocktail all night. He wondered what level of pain would greet the lifting of his head from the pillow. Answer: car crash. Instead, he slumped backwards and turned onto his side facing the bedroom door. He closed his eyes again and tried to piece together what had happened.

He remembered Destiny coming back from closing up at the club where she worked. He remembered him joining her for several large tumblers of Greek turpentine. He remembered the swirling melodies of Kula Shaker. But the freshest memory appeared to be Destiny's crop top and its loosely confined contents.

Craig put his arms under the duvet to check his state of undress below the waist. Relieved but not altogether surprised, his boxer shorts were still where they should be, albeit slightly crinkled. He hadn't apparently succumbed to temptation. And Craig would've remembered succumbing to the kind of temptation Destiny was packing, he felt sure of that. Well, 90% sure at least.

A glance at his watch informed Craig he had one hour before he was supposed to be attending a presentation about half a mile away. His holdall was not in the room. He suspected it was still by the lounge door where he had dumped it when he arrived. No tooth brushing had gone on last night. Anita wouldn't be impressed. She was a stickler for personal hygiene and gave Craig a hard time because he didn't floss. Craig thought that the ouzo could probably take the enamel from his teeth so plaque would've stood no chance.

Anita.

She would probably be even less impressed if she knew her husband was sipping late night drinks with a scantily clad sexpot with a proclivity for bondage and North African furnishings. She might've imagined him tucked up in his hotel, preparing for another day of high powered business meetings, if she was imagining anything that involved Craig. Lately, she had been so preoccupied with her own professional challenges he had started to feel invisible.

Craig decided to concentrate on the positives. It had been a stroke of luck that Destiny had been in touch. Their chance meeting had saved him from a long wait in the cold. It had been lucky she had a spare room and lived nearby. Luckier still, she was fun, witty and very hospitable, even if her obvious disregard for dressing warmly had sent the odd mucky thought racing through his mind. He had survived unscathed, albeit with a bruised liver and rip-roaring headache.

The final hurdle was to iron a shirt, exit the flat with minimal awkwardness and find somewhere that did a mean line in triple espressos en route to his meeting. He'd tell the boys about all this over a few beers at next month's poker night and they'd applaud his adventurousness then take the piss out of his late-night restraint, knowing they would all have done exactly the same. Apart from Steve, he was an animal.

So the biggest challenge of the day, Craig concluded, was going to be getting his head off of the pillow and into the shower.

Craig allowed himself another thirty seconds of succour, listening keenly for evidence that Destiny and her captivating curves might be moving around the flat. Nothing. As he tuned into possible noises from outside the bedroom, the only sound that registered was the tick of the small clock on his bedside table.

Craig's motionless silence was then rudely interrupted by the cat jumping from the floor onto the bottom of the bed. It landed on top of his feet nestled under the duvet. Craig was tempted to kick the bloody thing back onto the floor. Instead, he used it as a cue to swing his legs round and onto the floor. He cupped his face in his hands and rubbed his stubble to try to rouse the senses. The cat meowed and commented by swinging its head round to lick its arse.

"It's alright for you, Mr Tiddles," Craig said playfully. "You can sit there playing the banjo and staring down your creepy Cat Goddess friend here. But some of us have got to get going and earn a crust." The stoic porcelain edifice stared impassively back.

Craig exited the room and walked gingerly down the corridor scratching the contents of his boxers from the outside. He looked self-consciously down towards the carpet as he padded along the corridor. He glanced up to see the door to the lounge partly shut, obscuring its contents, but Destiny's bedroom door was open.

In a deep, gravelly and crackly voice he called out, "Just going to take a quick shower, if that's ok?"

Nothing. Craig stopped on his way into the bathroom but decided instead to creep along the corridor to find out if he was alone and could relax more.

Craig leaned into Destiny's bedroom.

"Hellooooo," he called without conviction. The room looked exactly as it had when he first viewed it. The bed was made and the handcuffs were where he had first noticed them. Craig rocked back onto his heels to withdraw the top half of his body back into the corridor, concluding that his hostess had already left the flat.

He pressed on into the lounge and pushed at the door, starting to walk in with head bowed and was immediately unnerved as the carpet felt wet against his bare feet. He lifted his left foot from the dampness and raised his head to peer across the room.

He was met by a scene that would forever be burned into his retinas.

Face down on the sofa was the figure of a woman. Her crop top had ridden up to reveal her milky white torso. In the middle of her back were two deep puncture wounds, both about 5cms long, running parallel to her spine, one either side, the one to the left slightly higher, halfway down her back. Both wounds looked like neat incisions without ragged edges. From each one trailed a line of blood, the width of the cut, running across the girl's back and onto the sofa where it had pooled and was dripping very slowly onto the brown patterned carpet. Craig noticed he had not breathed since the sight met his eyes and his lungs inflated against a huge pressure from inside his chest. His gaze was locked onto the strange picture of the girl's back, with the two deep red lines contrasting against the pale pallor of skin.

Her crop top was around her neck. Craig blinked which seemed to trigger a realisation that the body strewn across the couch didn't appear to be breathing. Craig noticed that his left leg was still raised from the carpet and, still staring at the girl, he returned it to the wet patch. The girl still had her black knickers on, and her legs were covered by long white knitted socks. The bottom of each sock was crimson.

Craig lifted his leg again, curled his foot upwards and looked down. His own foot was stained deep red.

Dazed and numbed, Craig looked back to the corpse on the couch and started to sense a building wave of panic emanating from the pit of his stomach. It was telling him to run, to take flight, an instinctive and overwhelming urge. But at the same time, Craig felt like his feet were rooted to the spot.

He raised his eye-line for the first time beyond the couch to the kitchen. The door was open and the stillness of the scene did not alert him to any imminent danger. Never in Craig's experience was the phrase 'deathly quiet' more apt.

It was at that second that, to his right, slightly obscured by the door which he was still holding open, Craig noticed something else. Or some*one* else, to be more accurate. A bare-chested black man was lying on the floor, face up. Both of his eyes were open but he lay perfectly still. This time, Craig noticed almost immediately that he was not breathing. There were no puncture wounds but the body was lying in a large pool of liquid soaked into the brown carpet. Craig noticed the pool had extended up to where he was standing. He looked back to the man's face and torso. Around his neck was a gold necklace which formed a 'v' shape down to a gold cross which rested on the man's breastbone. The gold cross was smudged by blood.

The sight of the second body seemed to spook Craig more than the first. The surreal picture of the first transfixed him. The second prompted a physical reaction. Craig turned around and started to bolt back down the corridor but his retreat was tripped up by the cat and he fell forwards, just managing to save himself from head-butting the corner of the radiator on the left-hand wall. Knocking himself out at a double murder scene was not a prospect that held much allure.

Craig raced back into the bedroom where he had roused himself not three minutes earlier. In such a brief passage, less than it took to toast a slice of bread, Craig's life had changed forever. And this realisation scared the fuck out of him.

Craig's mind was scrambled. He got dressed into last night's clothes at breakneck speed then, hyperventilating, he forced himself to sit on the end of the bed.

"Leave no trace," he said to the cat as it sauntered into the room. The brutal death of its owner seemed not to have registered particularly highly on the cat's list of current concerns. It sat on the floor and looked at Craig, as if judging his next move.

"What did you see?" Craig said to the cat. "I bet you saw the whole fucking thing." The cat responded by deciding it was high time for a huge yawn.

"Jesus fucking H. Christ," Craig said as he jumped up and frantically looked around the room for any sign of him having been there. He pulled the duvet over the bed and smoothed down the top surface to make it look unfettered. Having pulled the previous day's socks over his damp feet and slipped on his black shoes, he left the room.

He could not help but glance back towards the carnage of the lounge. His bloodied footprints, gradually fading in definition, walked towards him from the lounge. Where was his overnight bag? It had disappeared.

SUNSET OVER SUNSET © Steve Richards

He looked back into his bedroom then back out along the corridor and noticed it sat by the front door. He sprang towards it, mumbling frantic expletives under his breath.

He composed himself just enough to stop and try to remember if he had left anything in the flat. But his brain was porridge. He reached for the handle of the front door stopping just before he touched it to pull the sleeve of his jumper over his hand. He then pulled the catch to the right. He wiped the door catch with his jumper trying to polish away any fingerprints.

Before he fully opened the door, he paused again. He could not afford to meet anyone in the stairwell. That would be catastrophic. He thought further ahead and imagined his route away from the flat. He was in central London. CCTV cameras were everywhere. He needed to keep the lowest possible profile. Craig, still with his jumpered hand hovering above the door latch, looked to his right at the coat rack. On the nearest hook was perched a hat. Ideal. A-list celebrities had often been known to have negotiated packed airports unchallenged thanks to a cleverly positioned baseball cap and bowed head. Problem was that the hat on the hook closest Craig was not a baseball cap but a wide-brimmed straw hat complete with fetching pink band around the crown emblazoned in white capital letters with the phrase, 'Twatted in Tenerife'.

13
Spit & Polish

Pieter Pyptiuk enjoyed his work. He had arrived in London as part of the first modern-day wave of Polish immigrants a decade ago. Many of his countrymen and women had since returned to their motherland as the recession took hold, only to find their old jobs taken up by Indian immigrants.

Pieter had persevered. He endured the menial labouring jobs of the early years and then got a bar job at a late-night burlesque club called The Sunset. He liked to work late shifts. It gave him time to read and explore London's many distractions in the daytime.

Over the years he had made himself useful to Seamus, the club owner, doing odd jobs around the place as well as taking deliveries, running the bar, helping with staff issues and even getting involved in some of the book-keeping. The pay wasn't spectacular but the job suited Pieter. His handyman skills had also been invaluable to Seamus, a secretive man who trusted very few.

A year ago, the club's General Manager had left. There was no leaving do, no notice period, he simply didn't turn up for work one day and Seamus informed Pieter that Colin had 'departed for pastures new' after a few 'differences of opinion'. Pieter was asked if he could fill Colin's shoes. And without the faintest hint of a congratulations-on-your-new-job card, overnight Pieter had become GM of The Sunset and he was privately thrilled. He celebrated back in his tiny flat on Greek Street with a large bottle of Lucozade (sugar free).

Pieter rarely drank alcohol, a fact that helped to accelerate his departure from Poland where every man, woman and child seemed to drink like they were training for an Olympic event. Pieter was a natural introvert but when he hit his mid-twenties, he wanted to live in an area of the world where there was excitement. He didn't necessarily need to join in, he'd be more than happy to remain on the side-lines, but he needed to be somewhere where there was always something going on.

SUNSET OVER SUNSET © Steve Richards

The Soho area had, for decades, been the hub of late-night London with the sleazy reputation built in the twentieth century replaced more recently by a more diverse and rich diaspora. In Central London, Pieter had found his natural habitat.

Being smack in the heart of Soho, The Sunset Club attracted a wide range of colourful characters from London's varied cast. Gay people mixed with straight people who mixed with the tall, the short, the black, the white, the meek, the exhibitionists and the in-between. For the most part, there was a liberal attitude.

Pieter's relationship with the club owner had changed in recent months since he became the General Manager. He had been asked to take the reins on the nights when Seamus was out. That meant stashing the takings in the safe in Seamus's office, locking up and handling any incidental issues that arose. These mainly involved the club's performers or a group of rowdy blokes acting like pricks or, on the odd occasion, people overtly taking drugs. Pieter took care of things with no fuss. Front-of-house ran like clockwork, in no small part to the help of Destiny, the bar manager.

Destiny and Pieter got on famously from the start. She teased him for his quiet reserve and their skills complemented each other seamlessly. Destiny had been a dancer at the club when Pieter joined and he had assumed that Destiny and Seamus were an item, especially when the former hung up her tail feathers and was promoted to bar manager.

Destiny was smart. She had a knack for sensing problems before they arose and her flirty vivaciousness won over the staff and the punters alike. She was a force of nature, the heartbeat of the club.

Pieter had noticed that in recent weeks, Seamus had become more agitated. His impatience threshold had rarely been lower. Conversely, business at the club had rarely been better. Takings were up. Staff troubles were down and Pieter had thought his boss's mood should've been rosy. He was not naive enough to know that Seamus was involved in other 'business interests'. And he was smart enough to realise that these interests were not entirely the right side of legal. But Pieter respected Seamus's business acumen and he was loyal - especially when he remembered it was Seamus who had given him his big break and took him off the building sites to apply his talents more profitably.

So when Seamus had asked Pieter to wire the chair opposite his desk with a live electrical current, Pieter preferred to ponder the practical challenge rather than wonder about the practical use. He was mindful he could be criminally implicated if someone was to be seriously hurt, but Pieter's electrical know-how afforded him a degree of protection - no-one would be killed by the chair, he would see to that. (Unless the person sitting there had a serious heart defect or was pregnant but a Health & Safety warning notice probably wasn't an option.)

Pieter rose early this particular Thursday morning. He was going to take in the Victoria & Albert museum after breakfast following a recommendation from one of The Sunset's regulars. Over the years, Pieter had visited almost all of the cultural landmarks London had to offer. It bemused him how so many stunning exhibitions, works of art and antiquities seemed to be largely ignored by the local population. To Pieter, London was a treasure trove of wonders and most of the venues were free to get in. The jewel in the crown was the British Museum and Pieter went early to avoid the crowds of tourists. He must have visited a dozen times in the last year alone but today it was the turn of Victoria and Albert to divulge their curiosities and Pieter attacked his poached eggs with excited relish.

He came into work mid-afternoon. The club didn't open until 6pm but Pieter liked to be organised and prepared. His first hour was spent doing any odd jobs and the second involved him ordering any supplies and monitoring stock behind the bar. Thursday tended to be the second busiest night of the week and this evening a new singing and dancing act - The Rivelinoes - were to make their debut.

The evening's headline act usually went on at 10.30pm, preceded by dancing girls in various states of undress. Each girl, or team of girls, had an act – The Sunset was no run-of-the-mill strip bar. Some sang, some danced, some performed with props that ranged from snakes to budgerigars. One did all of the above until one of the snakes got into the basket holding the budgies and overnight she became a snake-only act.

One of the regular performers had left the previous evening to go back to Australia so Pieter spent his first half hour designing an ad for

SUNSET OVER SUNSET © Steve Richards

a replacement on his laptop. He printed off two copies on A3 paper and put one by the stairs and the other in the dressing room. Most of his recruits came from referrals from the existing acts. Pieter had heard horror stories from some of the other seedier bars in the area but Seamus treated his girls well on the whole. They were paid on time and received slightly over the odds.

The clientele was eclectic, to say the least, so entertaining such a wide range of tastes was a constant challenge. The general rule was that, as long as the act had no mainstream popularity or appeal, they stood a chance.

Pieter helped himself to a Red Bull. He was tired after spending hours feasting his eyes on the visual smorgasbord served up by the V&A. Thursday nights could get pretty racy and he had a feeling tonight was going to be one of those nights.

14
Hats Off

Anita McGill was irritable. Her alarm clock's battery had run out during the night and her body clock had failed to rouse her at her usual time of 5.45am. She would now have to rush to be the first one in the office. This was her trademark - to steal a march on her colleagues and impress the bosses by turning up while the lark was still under its duvet.

The tactic had stood her in good stead in the early days. It helped to get her noticed. She always had a natural, burning desire to achieve, to run rings around her peers. In recent months, however, her rise through the ranks at the solicitor's firm had stalled. She feared she had reached the glass ceiling, with further advancement blocked by her age, experience and the reluctance of the senior male colleagues to have a talented young woman invade their cosy world born of gender, nepotism and privilege.

Anita's mood was further darkened by the lack of milk available for her All Bran. Craig had probably drunk the whole pint before he left for London the day before. He could be an inconsiderate bastard at times. He was now away in London almost every week. Over the last two years, with Anita investing more and more thankless hours into her career, the meals out and occasional trips to the cinema had dried up. These had acted as a reset button for their relationship - a chance to catch up and reconnect.

Anita had avoided these instances in recent months as they would inevitably precipitate a discussion around children. Craig wanted kids but Anita knew a pregnancy would derail her rise to the top. It would give the bosses an excuse to overlook her. And she was not about to make it easy for them. She did want kids eventually but a blinkered focus on work was sensible and necessary in the short-term. Craig would just need to bear with her.

He could do with some of the same drive and determination, she thought, to kick-start his own professional aspirations. He didn't seem

SUNSET OVER SUNSET © Steve Richards

to care as much as he used to. It frustrated Anita. They didn't need the extra money but she found it difficult to understand his lack of desire. When she had married him, she thought their ambitions had burned equally brightly. He just didn't seem as driven lately and she worried that something was wrong. Not physically, although he had started to drink more than she thought sensible. He seemed less attentive. She didn't distrust him although nagging seeds of doubts were fed and watered whenever he stayed over in London.

Anita buried such thoughts and focussed instead on her toast and jam. But as a precaution, she had loaded an app on his phone that tracked his whereabouts. It would prove invaluable if it was ever stolen. He would thank her. It could lead the police straight to the culprits. And in the meantime, she could double-check to see if he did actually go to visit his mother on the outskirts of London on the Thursday afternoon before flying home, as he'd told her he would.

About four hundred miles south, Anita's husband was not particularly pre-occupied with the state of the apps on his mobile. He was more concerned about the imminent possibility of losing his mind.

Now outside the flat, his instincts screamed at him to contact the authorities immediately. Two people had been brutally murdered and it was his civic duty to report it as soon as possible. But three problems sprang to Craig's addled mind.

Firstly, he would be the prime suspect. He was the only other person at the murder scene, with no signs of forced entry. There was no murder weapon obviously apparent but he was the one stranger who had sprung from nowhere to intrude on these people's lives. Secondly, he thought back to the fateful 'friend request' on Facebook. It wouldn't take long for any self-respecting investigator to check Destiny's social media activity and spot the connection. This would not look good whether Craig flagged the crime or not, but he needed to buy some time to think and the power of making effective, clear decisions in the presence of fresh corpses was not in Craig's locker.

Finally, if he went straight to the police there was a good chance his

SUNSET OVER SUNSET © Steve Richards

marriage was over. He felt Anita was starting to get suspicious about his trips to London and news of him having a cosy sleepover with an 'old friend' who happened to be a sexy, unattached ex-burlesque dancer with a penchant for S&M would not allay her concerns. She would go mental.

So Craig bought himself some thinking time at a cost of having to sport a straw hat around Soho on a rainy Thursday morning in March. Craig was petrified of being filmed on CCTV leaving the flat. If he wasn't prepared to call the police immediately, leaving the flat in broad daylight would not look good. In fact, Soho was one of the few places in modern mainland Britain where you could just about get away with any kind of eccentric sartorial predilection without people stopping in the street and pointing at you.

He shuffled along quickly, holdall in hand, trying to remember if he'd left anything incriminating in the flat that could lead the police directly to him. In his haste he congratulated himself, mildly given the circumstances, for remembering his phone charger. He had left two in hotel rooms already this year when he comparatively had all the time in the world to retrieve them.

Craig intermittently stole a glance from behind the straw brim to check for cameras mounted on lampposts. He couldn't go into a coffee shop with straw hat in hand for fear of redefining the word 'conspicuous'. Instead he wound his way through some of the back-doubles he had learned to navigate in recent years and instinctively made his way towards his business meeting which was due to start in fifteen minutes.

Was this the best policy? Try to go on as normal? If he missed his meeting questions might be asked. He could cancel at short notice but his colleague would want to know the real reason at some point for having to take the strain. Craig found a relatively quiet lane near Great Titchfield Street and sat down on a table outside an unopened pub. He put his holdall on the bench alongside him, took off his hat and mopped his brow. He realised he was 'sweating like a Scouser in a library' as his friend Steve liked to say. Last night's poker evening suddenly seemed to Craig like it had occurred several decades ago.

As he tried to gather his wits, Craig's nagging doubt resurfaced that he'd left something obviously incriminating at Destiny's flat. He closed his eyes

SUNSET OVER SUNSET © Steve Richards

and visualised each of the rooms. He had double-checked the bedroom where he had slept. He had not spent any time in Destiny's bedroom. He had popped into the kitchen twice but only to top up his glass.

His glass. His DNA would be on the glass.

He had watched enough US crime dramas to know the forensic teams could track down people from a single nasal hair. Craig had never been charged with anything though. Could the authorities have his DNA anyway? Probably not but they could soon request it from the last person who had digitally befriended the girl before she was murdered.

For the first time, Craig seemed to realise the finality of what he'd seen. He stared blankly into space. Destiny was dead. A young woman, full of life, humour and energy would not be doing anything ever again. He thought back to their late night discussions after her return from the club. She had dressed flirtatiously but he didn't get the impression that this was particularly aimed at him. He assumed this was her style. It fitted her sassy personality. They had not really covered any meaningful background during their chat. She had struggled to find work after being laid off by the research lab where she had worked for a while. She was single after having been in a long relationship and wanted to have more fun. So she moved to central London and got talked into joining a burlesque dance troupe. She had loved it. She loved the fact it was risqué without being too seedy. She loved the camaraderie of the troupe. She liked the weird and wonderful characters she had met and she seemed to have loved her lifestyle.

But as Craig searched for more memories from the clouds of ouzo-induced fog he realised she hadn't spent a lot of time talking about herself. She had deflected conversation to try to find out what he had been up to. By comparison, his story was dull but she had not been judgemental. She had been easy to talk to, he recalled, no doubt aided by several neat tumblers of clear alcoholic spirit. He hadn't felt uncomfortable in his unfamiliar surroundings. He didn't feel she was seriously coming on to him and it wasn't particularly awkward when a modicum of sense entered proceedings and Craig decided he should go to bed before he made a fool of himself.

He thought back to when he had bumped into Destiny outside the hotel

SUNSET OVER SUNSET © Steve Richards

and remembered thinking it was a little too coincidental. Even after several beverages at poker night, he had hesitated before agreeing to shun the offer of the cab and follow her home.

A sense of heightened panic then struck Craig as he realised the straw hat had been a waste of time - any CCTV cameras would've spotted him with Destiny on their walk home the previous night. True, it would have been dark but the straw hat had been a stupid mistake. If anything it now made him look more culpable, if that was possible.

A moment of calm descended over him. He knew his decisions of the next half an hour would change his life forever. If he was going to contact the police it needed to be right now. He could explain his panicked, straw-hatted flight. He could explain how he had come to be at the flat. He could explain how the alcohol had knocked him out so he hadn't heard the intruder enter the flat or commit the murders. He was assuming there was another third party involved. Obviously the dead black guy had entered the flat after Craig had hit the sack but he assumed he had not stabbed Destiny then stabbed himself in the back.

A shiver ran down Craig's spine. This person had killed two people in cold blood, without fuss and with no evidence of huge struggle. The victims must have known him. If there had been lots of shouting and screaming Craig might've woken up. It suddenly dawned on him that if he had wandered out of his room to find out what the fuss was about, he would be lying in that lounge with Destiny and her friend. The realisation hit Craig like a kick in the stomach. Even if he hadn't woken up, Craig thought, if the murderer had noticed his overnight bag and suspected someone else was in the flat Craig would have been stabbed where he slept.

The sickening thoughts chilled his blood. But it helped him to come to a decision. He suddenly knew what to do. He had to phone the police. The prospect triggered another wave of nausea. His head hurt. He reached towards his bag – his trusty Nurofen capsules would take the edge off. As he unzipped, he immediately saw the brown, grease-stained paper bag holding his chicken McNuggets from the night before.

"For fuck's sake," he cursed as he retrieved the bag and threw it with disgust and annoyance backwards between his legs. 'How the fuck had he let it come to this?' he thought. He should be at his meeting any minute. He had to call the police. Now. His headache intensified. He reached back into his bag feeling inside for the inside zip. In the way, he felt something unfamiliar, hard.

He gripped it and pulled it out: a huge blood-strained hunting knife.

15
Rekindling

John Randwick had never been a fan of having meaningful conversations over the phone. He had seen too many phones tapped during his lines of enquiry to trust their security. He had been mulling over the best approach to reignite Nick Sands' interest in coming back to work. The previous day had provided a bite, today it was time to reel him in.

Randwick appreciated that his right-hand man had suffered two metaphorical kicks in the teeth large enough to keep the average dentist up to his elbows in spittle for months. Sands had initially bounced back well from the death of his lovely wife but the stabbing a few months ago had really set him back. The department had covered well for the most part. Resources were always stretched thinly but the workload over the first half of the past year was manageable.

The main trend on Randwick's patch had been the growing number of street robberies, especially late at night, perpetrated by well-drilled small teams of thieves and pickpockets from Eastern Europe and North Africa. Since the recession, tourism had fallen in the traditional havens of Barcelona and Rome. London had suffered a drop in the number of tourists too but not to the same extent. And there were still lots of rich, champagne-quaffing bankers ripe for getting ripped off after midnight as they tottered about searching for the most endangered of species after midnight, a black cab.

These crimes were mainly handled by the regular police force. When particular gangs were repeatedly culpable, Randwick's department was alerted and he was tasked to do something to boost the all-important crime stats.

On the violent crime front, things had been relatively quiet. Randwick had learned over the years that his realistic goal was not to eradicate gangland crime. That was like chasing rainbows. Gangs had existed from the beginning of human history and as long as human nature was turned on by power, danger and greed, Randwick knew that the

SUNSET OVER SUNSET © Steve Richards

gangs would endure. Periodically, there would be a spate of violence, usually triggered by a new gang trying to join the game uninvited, or by a new character joining one of the gangs who was keen to establish reputation. Occasionally a gang would splinter and there would be a squabble between the factions. In Randwick's lengthy experience, these evolutions were cyclical. Sure, in recent decades, the cast of major players had a more international flavour but they still knew where their respective boundaries were, and they all saw the benefit of not going out of their way to rattle the police's cage too much.

When members of the public got hurt, this was a different matter but the main growth in recent years had been around human trafficking and the supply of cocaine. London's drug habit had boomed since the Millennium. Demand was high and Randwick was aware of all of the key players trousering most of the cash.

Few were locals. The main players in central London were the Russians, who tended to supply the top-end business fraternity, the Albanians, who supplied most of the nightclubs and the Jamaicans who supplied the bars and clubs with softer drugs. In the outskirts of London there were numerous, mainly localised, players who were not Randwick's concern.

Since the turn of the year, the Blanchard crew from south London had been making some noise. They had been around for decades under the guidance of patriarch, Donny, but his son, Donald, had added some fresh impetus and they were mopping up some of the extra demand for cocaine around Randwick's patch. Recently the Blanchards had had a tussle or two with the Jamaicans but it had not escalated into a full-blown war, because that would draw too much attention and interrupt profits.

Everyone seemed to leave the Russians to get on with it but Donald Blanchard had been getting more ambitious lately and treading on a few more toes. There had been a few knife-fights and one shooting. Two members of the public had been hospitalised.

By chance, the daughter of Randwick's boss had been in the bar when the most recent shooting took place. One gang member had been rushed to St Thomas's and had lost a leg. Predictably, the man knew nothing about who might have done it but he was Albanian and Randwick sensed Donald's involvement as a public show of intent. Randwick had contacted Donald's father directly to tell him to calm his son down as the Chief Commissioner had taken a personal interest.

But there was something else that was concerning Randwick. Each of the main crews was slowly expanding to meet some of the extra demand for narcotics but they were limited in their supply lines. Randwick sensed someone else was getting involved. And it unnerved him that no-one was talking about who this new player might be. He didn't even know for sure that they existed at all but 20 years of experience gave Randwick a good feel for the game he was supposed to be marshalling. His instinct told him it was the same gang who had taken out his colleague and seriously injured Nick Sands a few months ago but evidence was painfully thin.

So he needed a fresh perspective and a fully-fit Sands was the ideal man. Even in a well of depression, Randwick knew Sands would provide a useful sounding board. The last thing Randwick needed was to be blind-sided by a new player, especially when the boss was taking a special interest.

He rang the doorbell of Sands' flat and stood back. Nothing. He rang again but there were no lights on and there was no movement from inside. Randwick tried a different tack and dialled Sands' mobile number. Listening intently in the quiet side street, he could faintly hear the ringtone through the front door.

"Nick, it's John."

"I know." Sands sounded non-plussed.

"I'm here. Outside."

"I know," Sands repeated.

"Well, come on," Randwick's irritation was rising, "open the door and let's get started."

But Sands was having second thoughts.

"Look, John, I'm not sure about this. I thought you'd turn up at my house rather than call but I'm not ready to dive back in the pool quite yet. I'm sorry you had a wasted journey."

Randwick sensed he was going to hang up and jumped in quickly. "Nick, Nick, don't go. Give me two minutes. I promise to leave you alone. Just give me a couple of reasons face-to-face, as I'm here and then you can be rid of me."

Silence. Randwick pictured his colleague in the room ten metres away. He began to doubt this was going to be worthwhile even if he did get his audience.

The line went dead. Randwick stared through the glass in the front door. He waited for another ten seconds then turned to walk back to his car. At the last second he noticed a light being turned on in the hallway and a blurred shape shuffling slowly towards him from inside the house.

Sands opened the door. He looked terrible.

"Two minutes," Sands said without looking Randwick in the eyes and turned around to wander back along the corridor.

16
See No Evil...

Pieter Pyptiuk was surprised to see his boss at four o'clock in the afternoon. Seamus rarely arrived at The Sunset before eight. From behind the bar, Pieter watched the diminutive, slightly-built Irishman strut purposefully from the stairs across the main floor and down the short corridor that lead to his office. He had known Seamus for long enough to recognise that type of walk as a 'don't bother me now' instruction.

After ten minutes or so, Pieter decided he would give him a try.

He knocked lightly on Seamus's office door and listened intently for a signal from inside but got no response. He thought he could faintly hear one side of a telephone conversation. He turned to walk away when something told him to be more persistent. He knocked again with more conviction on the heavy door.

Again, nothing. Pieter leaned in close and thought he heard Seamus's voice taking part in a hushed but urgent conversation but he couldn't quite make out the words. Pieter pressed his left ear to the door and almost immediately it swung open. Pieter tried to disguise his eavesdropping with a confident, "Ah, there you are, boss. Was just coming to see you."

Seamus looked flushed, the small capillaries in his cheeks standing out, angry against the pasty pallor of his face. He gave Pieter a knowing grin.

"A more perceptive boss than me might have suspected you had your ear pressed up against this door just before I opened it," said Seamus with a dead-eyed glare. "A more perceptive man than me," he continued, "might wonder why his manager might think it appropriate to interrupt him when he was so obviously busy."

Pieter dropped his gaze to the floor deferentially. "A cleverer boss than me," rasped Seamus, injecting menace, "might start to suspect that his manager hadn't learned a FUCKING thing in the last year about when - and when NOT - to bother him."

SUNSET OVER SUNSET © Steve Richards

Pieter looked his boss in the eye from under a furrowed brow, a look that showed the intimidating tone was having the desired effect.

"So, Pieter," Seamus sniffed theatrically at the air, "my nose is telling me that the club is not on fire. But my ears are telling me that your insistent knocking means there's something urgent to discuss. My eyes seem to have discovered a man who is keenly intent on listening to private conversations and this makes me feel very uncomfortable."

Pieter reverted to his intent study of the stone tiling by his feet.

"So, you see, Pieter, my senses are slightly skewed here. I wonder what you would make of it all if you were in my position?"

Pieter started a reply, "Well, it was ju..."

Seamus interrupted him with venom, "I don't give a flying FUCK at a rolling doughnut, what you were 'just' coming here to find out. What I need you to do, my Polish friend, is to do what you're paid to do and leave me the fuck alone to manage my affairs." He looked over Pieter's shoulder. "Now where the fuck is Destiny? I need to speak to her..."

"That's just it, boss" Pieter whined, "Destiny's disappeared."

SUNSET OVER SUNSET © Steve Richards

17
Train Hard

"Hello, it's me. Sorry for phoning you at work."

"Craig," said Anita, surprised as she sashayed through the office so she could talk privately into her mobile. She always deemed it terribly unprofessional to take personal calls in the main office in front of some of the juniors.

"Everything ok?"

"Yes, yes," piped Craig, desperately trying to keep it together. "Good news and bad news, though."

"Ok..." Anita's voice had turned from mild concern to suspicion.

"Well the good news is that we've had a really good new business meeting and I think I might have just nailed my quarterly target in one go."

"And the bad news...?" Anita said urgently.

"Well, they want me back tomorrow to speak to the boss. It's all very last minute." Craig shut his eyes and, just once, wished Anita would understand, trust his judgment and be happy for him. The length of the pause on the other end of the line did not, however, bode well.

"So you won't be home 'til Friday, is that what you're telling me, Craig?"

"Well, yes, bu..."

"Another night on my own," Anita interrupted, now safely alone in the kitchenette away from any eavesdropping. "Another night when you're running around London getting up to god knows what. Another..."

Craig pulled his mobile away from his ear and slid it down to rest by

SUNSET OVER SUNSET © Steve Richards

his chest. He knew this scenario all too well. Anita would whip herself into a frenzy and verbally knock his block off. This time, however, he didn't have the time or inclination to listen. He lifted the phone back alongside the side of his face and said, quickly, "Sorry, can't be helped," and disconnected. Anita had still been squawking on the other end but Craig knew he had bigger things to worry about. He pictured her at her office, holding the mobile away from her face, staring at it in disbelief at his rudeness.

On discovering the bloodied hunting knife in his bag, Craig had panicked. He immediately shoved it deep back inside his holdall, stood up and set off towards the Thames. He knew that if he was discovered in possession of what he assumed was the double murder weapon, having not called the police and snuck around central London in a straw bloody hat, he would be locked up never to re-emerge.

His instincts told him to get to the river and get rid of the knife. But these were the same instincts that had compelled him not to call the police and instead to flounce around central London in broad daylight looking like a drug-addled raver with six congealed McNuggets and a blood-stained hunting knife in his bag. At this rate, Craig was going to fall out entirely with his instincts. They had betrayed him just when he needed them to behave themselves and do what good instincts should do - tell his scrambled brain what the fuck to do.

So how was he going to slip a large knife into a huge river in mid-morning in one of the world's most densely populated cities in the world? A brief moment of calm washed over him. He needed to think straight. How long did he have before the bodies would be discovered? Craig knew Destiny worked at a burlesque club. They didn't usually open until, say 8pm, so she wouldn't be expected at work until maybe 7pm at the earliest. They might call her if she was late but they wouldn't necessarily get worried and raise the alarm immediately. This gave him some time.

But Destiny was the outgoing sort. She might well have arranged to meet someone that morning who would be worried when she didn't turn up or answer her phone. If her friend or friends lived nearby they might stop by the flat to find no answer. Who else might have a key? Well, it seemed like the Rasta man might have had one as Craig didn't hear a doorbell before he nodded off into his ouzo-induced coma.

SUNSET OVER SUNSET © Steve Richards

Craig dwelled for a moment on the bare-chested man sharing Destiny's lounge. His face, with unstaring eyes, looked vaguely familiar but Craig couldn't quite place him. Had he been in the pub where they'd been playing poker? Had he been a spotter for Craig all along and tipped off Destiny so she could fortuitously bump into him on purpose. Had he been set up? No, that didn't make any sense as the people setting him up were both now growing cold in a basement flat and he was still ok. Well, not exactly ok. Mentally mangled and physically shot-to-pieces, but his body was at least still functioning as a going concern.

Craig was roused from his reverie by a rumble in his pocket. His text read:

"Hello. All ok? I'm of shoping with your Aunte Lorna. Hop u and Annita r ok. Spake later. Mum x"

The mundane, misspelt, mistyped normality of the text made Craig instantly yearn for a world where he would be digesting his breakfast in a mind-numbing business meeting rather than lurking around London with a murder weapon that now featured his fingerprints.

The dose of reality also made Craig yearn for the company of his mum. In times of crisis, he had always turned to home, like when he failed his cycling proficiency test or got an unexpected fine at the library. With the nurturing help of home, Craig had managed to come to terms with just this kind of crushing setback and move on with his life. As setbacks go, however, his current predicament even had the potential to outweigh the seriousness of Craig's infamous dropped catch in the 1988 school cricket finals which had saw him thrown off the team and 'chucked' by Lucy Blackhurst, the girl with the best legs he had ever seen, before or since.

Craig clicked his phone off. The text had provided renewed impetus. He would head for London Bridge station and take the suburban overland train, "calling at New Beckenham, Clock House and Elmers End". Craig knew he must run the gauntlet to try to get home before his mother headed to M&S Food for her habitual Thursday afternoon latte with Auntie Lorna.

The rush hour was over by the time Craig reached London Bridge. He had never noticed before, but there was a large police presence around. Ok, some of the uniformed officers were transport police and others were Community Support Officers. And some were ticket inspectors, but in Craig's parlous state, anyone vaguely dressed in any official-looking uniform presented a heart-jumping imminent threat of discovery, capture, incarceration and almost inevitable non-consensual buggery.

From a young age, Craig often had dreams where he was in prison for some dastardly crime he didn't commit. Watching episodes of 'Porridge' on TV with his dad as a kid, jail had seemed nothing more than a mild inconvenience at worst. All you had to do was 'keep yer nose clean' and avoid Harry Grout. At times it seemed like the inmates had quite a laugh if your cell-mate happened to be Ronnie Barker.

Craig's youthful dreams had involved him eluding the long arm of the law until he had mistakenly spoken in English at a German train station like poor old Gordon Jackson in The Great Escape. In more recent times, gritty TV dramas and a plethora of harrowing films had done their best to rearrange this rose-tinted view and Craig was under no illusion of what awaited him if things went badly in the next few hours. And he knew himself well enough to know he was not ready - emotionally or physically - for a game of 'Where's the Soap?' at Wormwood Scrubs with 'Scabby Alan', the amorous ex-cage fighter from Hull.

As he bought his rail ticket, Craig became aware of the heavy holdall and stiffly held it in his right hand, trying his best to look natural as he negotiated the slope that led to the platforms. The train he needed was just about to pull away when he reached the platform and a last-ditched sprint for the electronic doors saw Craig leap onto the train just in time. Unfortunately his holdall fared slightly less well and it was now wedged between the doors, stuck fast. Craig frantically tugged at the bag's handles but the strain of all the pulling and the pressure of the doors was starting to unpeel the main zip, exposing its contents. Another strong tug and Craig anticipated the bag's contents spilling half inside and half outside the train. Craig caught a glimpse of his fresh white shirt starting to emerge from the bag. It was stained with blood. He looked through the train doors' windows and noticed the guard from the opposite platform jogging towards him. The high-pitched bleeps of the door alarm rattled around Craig's skull and sweat poured from his brow. Then the alarm suddenly stopped, the doors re-opened and the freed bag swung towards him. He quickly closed the zip and the guard gave him a laconic shake of the head through the window before holding

SUNSET OVER SUNSET © Steve Richards

his white paddle aloft to send the train on its way.

Craig spun his head both ways to look down the carriage. Thankfully it was quiet. He was going in the opposite direction to the last wave of straggling commuters, against the rush hour traffic. The only other person in the carriage, however, a thick-set black man in his early thirties looking stoically cool in wraparound sunglasses, was staring straight at him.

Craig shuffled in the opposite direction and took the furthest away seat at the end of the carriage. The mental pressure was starting to tell. He'd only been up three hours but he was suddenly desperately tired. The incident with the doors and the menacing eye-witness had sapped his fragile reserves. His resilience was faltering. Craig pondered defeat. He took out his phone and resolved to text his mother to tell her he was coming. After typing the first word, his eye was drawn to the front-page headline of the free newspaper left on the seat next to him:

'FBI Hacker Goes Rogue'.

Craig looked back at this phone and held it with suspicion. People could track his texts. Anything he broadcast could possibly implicate him later. No one could be sure what the government, FBI, or even bloody Tesco for that matter, was tracking.

He started to delete the word when his eye was drawn to the large frame of the man in the shades looming towards him. Craig hunched down slightly, trying to make himself invisible but the man kept on coming. No-one else had entered the carriage. He had to be coming for him. As he got closer, he noticed the guy's shoulders. They were huge. There was no way Craig was going to fight a man with this physique. Then he noticed his t-shirt under his jacket. It seemed to be emblazoned with a biker gang's logo.

Craig unzipped the top of his bag, pushed his hand in and grasped the hilt of the hunting knife. It felt reassuring. It could avoid him being caught. The man, now only three feet away, stopped and stared at him through the dark lenses. Craig was ready. Poised, armed and ready to defend himself. The train's brakes were applied and the man lurched forward slightly towards him.

SUNSET OVER SUNSET © Steve Richards

Craig was just about to remove the knife from the bag when he was distracted by a sudden movement at knee level. A dog. A Labrador in a hi-vis jacket. It must've been lying obscured from view at the man's feet when Craig got on. The man spoke in a high-pitched, upper-class accent;

"Hello? Is someone there? Could you possibly let me know if the next stop is Catford Bridge? I've rather lost track of the stations and the automatic announcements don't seem to be working."

Craig noticed the dog's jacket featured the words, 'Guide Dogs for the Blind'.

"Hello? I think there is someone there," said the man, "I can sense you. Would you be awfully kind and do a good turn for a blind man?"

The train was slowing to a stop alongside the platform. Craig looked outside the window to see a 'Catford Bridge' sign rear into view.

Craig's voice cracked as he spoke. He released his grip on the knife.

"Oh, er, yes, er, sorry. Yes, this is Catford Bridge. Would you like me to, er, help..?" Craig stuttered, standing up to try to guide the man by the elbow back down the carriage toward the doors.

"Ah, no need, sir. Thanks so much for the tip-off. Sandy, here, can take the lead now. I'm pretty sure she can read," he reached down to pat the dog, "but she doesn't speak English!" Craig managed a half-hearted, stilted laugh.

The door alarm sounded, the man effortlessly reached the button to trigger it and turned his head.

"You've been awfully kind. Have a wonderful day." As he got off, he started talking to his dog, his voiced fading away, "What a kind, chap, Sandy. A total gent...."

Craig slumped back into his seat. He needed his mum.

SUNSET OVER SUNSET © Steve Richards

18
Never Go Back

Nick Sands had done very little but he was exhausted. He slumped into the armchair that had dominated his world in recent months to mull over John Randwick's visit.

Randwick had been clever. He had not spent any time trying to persuade Sands to come back to work. It was too personal, too confrontational. It was also needy and John Randwick was not about to beg anyone to do anything. Instead he had appealed to Sands' professional curiosity. And it had worked on one level in that Sands had enjoyed the mental stimulus. The part he had not liked was the personal nature of the case that was baffling his colleagues.

Randwick had shared his thoughts about the new player in the gangland fraternity. The problem was that no-one seemed keen to reveal who it might be. All of the usual avenues had been pursued; snitches and ex-cons looking for a quick buck in return for some useful information. Randwick had also taken the usual step of approaching a couple of longstanding contacts within the established crews that worked his patch and surrounding districts. It was apparent to these guys too that toes were being trod on and commercial markets were being encroached. Physical violence and injury was part and parcel of gangland operations and on the whole it was kept low-level to avoid too much scrutiny.

But what these gangs found more painful was being hit in the pocket. They tended to be highly geared: Lots of people to pay off, lots of outgoings and lots of lavish lifestyles to sustain. If turnover and margins were squeezed, just like any business operation, certain people tended to suffer. Unlike most business operations, however, the suffering in gangland London tended to involve people losing limbs.

Most new players didn't last long. They tended to come in with a bang and go out with a whimper. The established gangs had experience and they knew the lie of the land; where to buy, where to sell, who to pay off and how to deter unwelcome competition. But there was something different about this new crew.

Randwick explained to Sands that he had taken the unusual step of asking cockney kingpin Donny Blanchard for a heads-up. Who was causing trouble and why had the existing players not stamped on this new bug biting into their margins and stinging their bottom lines?

Donny had been uncharacteristically prickly when Randwick spoke to him. He always answered Randwick's rare requests to meet. They had to be invisibly private. They had to be off the record. But Donny had been running his show long enough to understand the value of having a contact in the right place. When they had met the day before, Randwick relayed that Donny had been rattled. Randwick could understand him being tetchy. His profitability was being adversely affected and he didn't like it.

Usually, Donny would have given him a point in the right direction and Randwick would have organised a bust or two to inconvenience the new player. Better the devil you know and all that. But even though Donny was unquestionably annoyed, he seemed unable or unwilling to pass on any details. He was not in the first flush of health but for the first time, Randwick sensed a weakness he had not seen before. Donny looked physically smaller; less confident and assured. Something - or someone - had got under his skin.

Randwick noticed he became even more irritable when he asked how his son, Donald, was doing. Donny was immediately defensive. Randwick wondered if Donald had been misbehaving. He had inherited his father's 'youthful exuberance' but Randwick sensed an emotion he had not associated with the Blanchards before now - worry. Despite his probing, however, Donny had stonewalled Randwick and the meeting yielded no immediate reward so he asked Sands for his perspective.

"Sounds like the new firm is unusually camera-shy," Sands offered, having listened in silence for almost twenty minutes.

Randwick gave him an encouraging nod.

"Sounds like they're organised too. To take decent chunks of the market, from several players, takes organisation but it also takes cast-iron confidence. This new crew means business and they sound like they're staying put. It also sounds like they've got old Donny Blanchard on the back foot which he won't like one little bit."

Four sentences. Not exactly Churchillian, bit it was the most Sands had said out loud to anyone but his son for eight months.

Randwick looked at him and leaned forward in his chair opposite. "Nick," he said, "I've got the feeling this one's going to get ugly. I could use you back in the team. The boys have been great covering for the last few months but this one is going to need all hands on deck."

He stood up. "But I'm not the nagging type so I'm going to leave it with you." He moved out of the lounge door. "I'll show myself out."

Randwick marched down the corridor towards the front door and knew he had done all he could to tempt Sands back into the fold. He wasn't going to force someone with Sands' recent history to rejoin when he sensed the next few days and weeks would be demanding and dangerous. It had to be Sands' call but he sincerely hoped he would make the right one - one that would see him back in the office as soon as possible.

Back inside his lounge, Sands heard the front door slam behind Randwick and he sat motionless in silence. He had always liked working for Randwick. He had given him a break early in his career and he was fair and straight. He knew some of his counterparts in other CIDs weren't as morally perpendicular. Some were downright twisted. But Randwick always seemed to have a healthy respect for law and order and he also treated his team with respect and stuck up for them whenever they needed support.

As he sat slumped in his chair, Sands mused over the challenge facing his boss. He knew he could offer something, give the team a better chance of a positive result. But he also knew he was out of practice. Eight months or more of sitting in his lounge would mean he was physically and mentally adrift.

He also worried if the stabbing would make him hesitate at a vital moment and put a colleague in extra danger. He didn't really care much for his own personal safety. Since Smita's death, there had been times when he wished the assailant's knife hadn't missed all of those vital organs and he would now know for sure if the afterlife existed one way or another. In the dark days of recovery and reclusiveness, Sands had also toyed with heavy liquor. After all, a thousand and one senior coppers couldn't be wrong, could they? Drink helped you cope. A thin smile crept along Sands' lips as he remembered a phrase his grandfather had trotted out most Christmases when he was a kid: 'I'd rather have a full bottle in front of me than a full frontal lobotomy'.

Sands' fond memory was interrupted by the trill blast from his phone.

'Who now?' he thought irritably. After nothing for months, today was the equivalent of Piccadilly Circus on VE Day. He let it ring five times then picked it up. It was his brother-in-law, Anil.

"Hey, Mr Grumpy. How's it hanging?" he said playfully. "I've got someone who wants to talk to you…" Sands listened to the clicks and bumps down the phone-line as the handset was passed over. He knew what was coming.

"Hello, dad," came the young voice of Sam, his son. "Are you ok?" Sands detected genuine concern and pictured his son clutching the phone in the busy household of his extended family.

"I'm fine," said Sands, his voice suddenly and unexpectedly breaking with emotion.

"You ok, dad," said Sam urgently.

"Fine, son," said Sands, wiping away the tears that flowed involuntarily down each cheek. "Just fine. How are you? Why aren't you at school?" he asked, checking his watch, trying to deflect to bat back the conversation.

"Sore throat today. I was allowed to stay off," said Sam. A pause. "I got 18 out of 20 in my maths test yesterday."

Nothing was offered in reply. Sands' chest was convulsing as he suppressed the sound of his sobs.

"Dad?" Sam asked. "You still there?"

Sands swallowed hard. "I'm here, Sam, I'm here," he said, the emotion causing his tone to raise an octave. Sands took a deep breath. "Sam?" he said.

"Yes?" the young voice shot back, expectantly.

"How would you feel if your dad went back to work?"

"I think it would be a good thing," said Sam. He was a level-headed kid who had been through a lot for an 11 year-old. "It would make Anil happy, too."

Sands imagined Anil's face close to Sam's, breaking into a smile while trying to listen in to their conversation.

"It might be dangerous, though, Sam," said Sands. "Your dad has to deal with some people who are nasty and sometimes hurt people."

"Like Tom Scovell?" asked Sam. "He's a nasty boy in my class. He hasn't hurt me yet but he likes to pick on the smaller kids. I want to help them but then he will pick on me too."

Sands thought of the son he had been neglecting. It wasn't fair for him to have to deal with these everyday trials and tribulations of growing up without his father. It wasn't fair that Smita's family was filling the void. Sam needed his dad back in the picture and it was about time he stopped hiding himself away and grasped his responsibilities.

"There are lots of Tom Scovells out there, Sam," Sands said. "You must not let them intimidate you. You must use your brain to out-smart them and make them look small. It's not easy, son. Sometimes it might seem impossible. But there comes a time to stand up to the bullies and you will know when the time is right." Sands paused to let his advice sink in. He realised the advice was as much for himself as it was for his son.

"I think you should go back to work, dad," said Sam. "Don't worry about me. If Tom Scovell comes near me I'll kick him in the balls like you showed me."

SUNSET OVER SUNSET © Steve Richards

Sands let go a burst of laughter. "That's it, son. I'm proud of you."

"I'm proud of you too, dad," Sam said.

"I'll come and see you at the weekend, Sam. Now make sure you rest that throat but could you do one little thing for me in the meantime?"

"Of course, dad."

"Can you flick Anil in the ear and tell him to stop listening in to other people's conversations?"

Two laughs were returned down the phone line. Sands said his goodbyes then looked around for his coat. If he called quickly enough, Randwick might come back and give him a lift.

19
Mum's the Word

Craig managed to avoid further major incident for the ten minutes it took to get to his destination. It felt better to be away from the humdrum hullabaloo of central London. The streets were quiet as he wandered along, past the take-away *'Abra-kebab-ra'* and the off-licence, *'Thirsty Work'*. It was comforting to see familiar places although Craig found it difficult in his current quandary to raise a smile at either.

As he walked, he decided that the plan he had hatched on the train had potential so even though he was only 200 metres from his mother's flat, he jumped on the local bus. He had an errand to run and he reckoned he just had time before his mother and Auntie Lorna got back to the flat having mercilessly attacked the fruit scones at M&S.

Just over an hour later, Craig stood outside his mother's low-rise block of flats. It was a relatively new building and was comfortable, if unremarkable. The family home in Scotland had been sold a few years earlier as 72 year-old Margaret McGill had found it difficult to maintain. It also contained too many memories of her husband, Iain, who had died suddenly after a heart attack a decade before. Margaret was originally from London and her daughter, Craig's sister, Moira, had settled down south with her City-banker husband and two small children in nearby Chislehurst. So after much thought and tearful farewells in Edinburgh, Margaret moved back down south to be near her grandkids.

Craig had felt this was a vote of no-confidence. His mother obviously believed there was no imminent prospect of Anita and him producing offspring. His sister was younger, in her late twenties, but already had two kids, delivered, weaned and now both were walking and talking. And Granny Margaret doted on them both.

Craig was pleased his mother had made some friends after moving at a reasonably advanced age. This had been helped by joining the local old people's club and continuing to provide advice to people at the local chapter of The Samaritans. Trips out with Auntie Lorna, an eccentric

SUNSET OVER SUNSET © Steve Richards

long-term family friend who was an aunty in an emotional rather than biological sense, also kept Craig's mum busy.

He had never before turned up unannounced but these were special circumstances, to say the least. The downstairs front door had been propped open so Craig climbed the communal staircase to the first floor. He was pretty sure she lived in number 14 but he had only visited a couple of times in the few years she had been here. As he walked past the other doors, a renewed sense of anxiety washed over him. He had not planned what he was going to say.

Did he really expect an elderly grandma, whose dose of danger rarely went beyond a double bill of *Deal or No Deal*, to be able to take an active part in extricating her son from the very deep hole he inhabited? She had always been good at providing practical advice but Craig was about to give her resourcefulness an Olympic-sized work-out.

When she found out what had happened and how he had reacted, he was pretty sure she'd be furious and insist he immediately contact the police. Craig's nervousness turned to pure panic when he saw that the front door to Flat 14 was slightly ajar. The picture of Destiny's face meeting him outside the hotel the night before flashed into his mind, replaced instantaneously by the image of her face-down lifeless body.

Since she was widowed, Craig knew that his mother had been particularly safety-conscious. She would not willingly have left her front door open. Something was wrong. A bolt of adrenalin coursed through his veins as he stood just outside the door, peering through the crack.

First thing he noticed was the aluminium baseball bat he had given his mother when his dad died. But as he squinted, he couldn't see anything else. He listened intently and heard muffled sounds coming from inside. The intruder was still there. Craig dropped his holdall at his feet and pushed the doorbell. Another noise from inside, followed by his mother's shrill voice calling "I'll be there in a moment".

Craig sensed an uncomfortable urgency in her voice so he pushed the door open and strode into the living room brandishing the baseball bat. A grey-haired man was stood in front of his mother with his back to the door.

SUNSET OVER SUNSET © Steve Richards

"Get away from her!" Craig shrieked in a tone he didn't recognise as his own.

As the man spun around Craig cocked the bat behind his head, ready to unleash a full swing at the man. In a split second, he looked past the man and noticed the top two buttons on his mother's blouse were undone and she was busily re-fastening them. He then noticed the grey-haired man was wearing a smart grey suit complete with crimson silk handkerchief in top pocket. These images combined to make Craig pause at the top of his backswing. He then glanced down instinctively at the elderly man's crotch and noticed a huge erection inside the man's trousers pointing directly at him.

"Craig!" his mother said urgently. "I'd like you to meet Clive. He's a close friend and I'd like it very much if you didn't batter his head in."

The man swung his head behind him to look at Margaret. "Craig?" he said. "As in..."

"Clive," interrupted Margaret, a coyness entering her tone, "I'd like you to meet my son, Craig.

Clive turned his head back to face Craig who lifted his gaze three feet to regain eye contact. Clive turned his head back and the two men stared at each other for a second without speaking. A fourth voice came from behind Craig, from the direction of the front door. It sounded like an elderly woman.

"Margaret! Everything alright?" Craig turned his head and the three of them stared at a plump woman in a housecoat holding a silver candlestick in her right hand.

Margaret stood up from the couch. Craig lowered the bat to his side.

"Oh, Prudence! There you are. What a to-do. I'm fine. Fine. Just an, um, misunderstanding." Prudence eyed both men suspiciously.

"Master McGill, in the drawing room with the baseball bat," said the man in the grey suit in a deep, rather posh voice, a smirk spreading across his face. "Murder most foul!"

SUNSET OVER SUNSET © Steve Richards

Prudence stared down at the elderly man's erection, bemused.

"Well," she said uncertainly, "I heard the scream and, well, the front door was open and I, well..." Margaret walked forward between the two men towards her latest visitor.

"You are just sooo kind, Prudence. And sooo brave. Whatever would I do without you?" Margaret ushered Prudence away from the group and back out towards the front door. She shut it with a loud 'clunk' and turned around to look back at the two men in her life who were staring at each other. "I really do need to get the catch on that door fixed," she said as she re-entered the room.

"Mum, what's going on? Who the hell is this bloke?"

"Now don't take that tone with me, Craig. You could have called first, you know. To say 'I wasn't expecting you' doesn't really do it justice." She straightened her blouse self-consciously.

"Well, who is he?" Craig repeated.

"He's a friend. As I said."

Clive decided it was time to chime in. "Quite a weapon, that," he declared, nodding towards the bat. "Lightweight model. Aluminium. Imagine you could knock someone's head off if you really wanted to. But immensely pleased you didn't swing it. Might've flattened the old schnozzle," he said reaching up to waggle the end of his nose with his right hand.

"Mum, I need to talk to you," Craig said seriously, staring at the carpet. He looked up, directly into her eyes, "It's important."

Margaret looked at Clive.

"Hey, don't mind me, old girl," trumpeted Clive, mildly amused. "I only popped round for tea and crumpet, don't you know."

Craig glared at him.

"Have you just walked off the set of some *Carry On* film," Craig hissed, his

SUNSET OVER SUNSET © Steve Richards

irritation boiling over. "Why don't you take your stupid little moustache, your stupid silk handkerchief and your fucking hard-on for a walk around the block. I need to speak to my mum, alone, NOW!"

"Craig!" shouted Margaret in dismay. She moved to stand more closely between them. "I can see you're upset, love, but that's no way to speak to one of my friends. Clive has been very good to me in recent months."

"I bet he has," Craig spat, "'tea and bloody crumpet', indeed." He wasn't in the mood for making new friends.

"Now that's ENOUGH, Craig!" chastised Margaret. She looked thoroughly shocked by her son's surly attitude and colourful language.

"Look, Margaret," Clive said, "I don't want to get in the way here. Bit of a stand-off. Roosevelt and Stalin at Yalta and all that. Totally understandable. I'll make sure I fully clunk the front door this time. Frightful imposition."

"I want you to stay, Clive," Margaret said solemnly to her son. "Craig here needs to find the manners I taught him and appreciate the situation. Clive is part of my life now so you're just going to have to get used to it."

Craig stared at her blankly. His batteries were running low. His shoulders slumped in defeat.

"Fine. Whatever. I just need…" he sat heavily onto the great sofa and rested his elbow on the arm which inadvertently triggered the mechanism that flicked the seat back. Craig shot back and a foot-rest sprang from underneath, lifting his legs. Margaret shrieked a hoot of laughter. "I say," muttered Clive.

"Clive," said Margaret caressing the elderly man's shoulder, "why don't you be a love and go and make us all a nice pot of tea. I think Craig might be having one of those days."

SUNSET OVER SUNSET © Steve Richards

20
Tortuous

"You see, you could say I'm having one of those days," said Seamus casually to the man sat in front of him.

"Staff not turning up to work, having to drop everything to sort out an unforeseen problem." He accompanied the final five syllables with gentle taps on the man's cheek, although the man in front of him was not in a position to say anything, bound as he was to the swivel chair with thick gaffer tape and his mouth taped shut by black tape wound several times around his head.

Seamus continued. "You see, I can cope with people letting me down. Staff nowadays can be unreliable. It's a generational thing. No respect for responsibility. People just don't care these days, Sergei."

"And it's a disease that might well bring western civilisation to its knees," he added, accompanying the final word with a crushing whack of his cylindrical ebony ruler into the man's left kneecap. The man's yelp was muffled by the tape. His face was flushed bright red. He looked angry rather than scared.

The man trapped in the chair was muscular, tall, lean and had a shaved head. In his left ear, he wore a diamond earring and a message in Russian script was tattooed on his neck behind his right ear. He fixed a murderous stare on Seamus who was flanked by four large men in balaclavas, two each side.

"Some people are unreliable, Sergei. It's a fact of life. I don't like it any more than you, my Russian friend. I try not to take it personally. But I take great care to work with people who know not to make that mistake. Trusted people. People who understand the importance of trust and reliability. People who keep their eyes..." he poked the man hard in the left eye with the end of the ruler, "...and ears..." he hit the man in the side of the head, "...open."

Blood trickled from the tear-duct of the injured eye. "People who understand capitalism and how open and competitive market forces work."

Seamus walked slowly behind the man in the chair who was now sweating profusely and blowing hard through his nostrils to disperse the pain, dislodging long streams of snot. He still didn't look particularly scared by his predicament but his anger had now escalated to a full-blown, volcanic rage.

In contrast, Seamus softened his tone and gently put his hands on the man's shoulders having handed the ruler to one of the balaclava'd henchmen.

"Now I happen to know that you know all of this, Sergei. You served manfully in Kosovo. You served Comrade Putin commendably a decade ago by bashing in Chechen heads. Loyalty and respect are not foreign values to a professional man like yourself." The man's breathing started to settle slightly.

"In another life, I think you and I might've got along." Seamus unfurled a canvas roll containing shining surgical implements. He carefully selected a scalpel and turned to face the back of the man's head. Sergei's resolve seemed to crumble slightly. He looked anxiously at the four pairs of expressionless eyes protruding from the holes in the balaclavas.

"The problem here," Seamus continued in softened tones, "is one of common decency." The man tried to swivel on the chair but it was stuck fast. "I can be a reasonable bloke, Sergei. I, too, am professionally trained," he swivelled the scalpel dextrously between his fingers. "We have both worked hard to achieve status in our respective fields." The man tried again to swivel and Seamus slapped him hard in the back of the head with his spare hand. "But today was not the day to provide me with an unforeseen circumstance. And hurting one of my ex-paramilitary men is strictly outside of the boundaries I can allow."

"Which is why you're here, Sergei. Boundaries and parameters and the preservation thereof." Seamus gave an almost imperceptible nod towards one of his men who immediately hurried away. A renewed level of concern shuddered through the man's body as his good eye flitted left and right.

SUNSET OVER SUNSET © Steve Richards

"Boundaries are what we all need to respect. It's important. Some would say a matter of life and death," Seamus said, coinciding the final word with a quick incision in the man's neck with a flick of his wrist. He immediately stood back quickly to avoid the plume of blood that started to shoot from the man's neck. Seamus looked towards another of his men and pointed to the roll of surgical instruments.

Without haste, the man walked over to an iPod and speaker doc set up next to a power point on the floor of the static caravan in the deserted building site. A tune familiar to the Irishmen started to fill the space.

Seamus shouted over his shoulder as he walked away, "Don't worry, Comrade Sergei. Help is on its way. Let's hope it gets here in time, though, eh. But the Ambulance Service is under severe pressure these days. It's cuts, cuts, cuts, for those guys."

Seamus continued to walk away, unable to suppress a smirk.

"Anyway, Sergei, as they say in Russia - 'Moscow.'"

Sergei fell unconscious, the pool of blood surrounding his seat getting bigger by the second.

SUNSET OVER SUNSET © Steve Richards

21
The Best Form of Defence

Margaret McGill and Major Clive Hackforth (ret'd) sat on the former's flower-patterned sofa. Silence reigned. They had just listened to Craig's account of the previous day. Margaret held her hand over her mouth and looked distraught, on the verge of tears. Clive looked like someone had just lit his touch-paper. He leaned forward, rubbing his hands, ready to spring into action.

"By jove, old thing. What a proper fix you've landed yourself in!"

He sounded almost amused. His perfectly trimmed grey moustache twitched. Craig glared at him. Having to recount the sorry tale of mishap, misdemeanour and murder gave his predicament a surreal tinge.

"Whatever to do?" Margaret murmured softly. Craig took her hand.

"I'm so sorry, mum. I just didn't know where to go or what to do." Craig gently shook his head. "I know. I should've called you to let you know I was coming but I saw this thing about phone hacking in the paper and I just thought..."

Margaret stood up and moved towards her son to give him a hug. His sister had provided the grandchildren which provided an abundance of joy for Margaret, but she had always had a special relationship with her first-born. They had understood each other from the start, cut from the same cloth.

"I'm such an idiot," Craig lamented.

"Now, then, young sir," Clive barked to shake him. "No time for self-pity. It's every soldier's worst enemy on the battlefield. Got to stay sharp. Got to stay alert and resolute in the face of crisis."

Craig simply stared at him implacably. Clive recognised the signs and swung into action. He stood and started to pace around the living room.

SUNSET OVER SUNSET © Steve Richards

"Now, I've heard a lot about you in recent months," he said, putting his hands together and pointing them towards Craig, who had removed himself from his mother's embrace.

"A helluva lot of good stuff, actually," continued Clive, now stroking his moustache with index finger and thumb of his left hand. "You're a resourceful chap, by all accounts. You have a jet-setting job. You have a clever and talented wife and a lovely house in Edinbro'. You've even been known to buy magazines from those chaps with dogs on ropes who seem to be on every street corner these days."

He stared out of the window into the middle distance while Craig forgave the typically English mispronunciation of his home town. "Marvellous city, Edinbro'," Clive declared, turning back sharply to face Craig.

"Superb history. Some very fine men have come from chilly Jockland in my experience. Some very fine men, in-deeeed." His whole ex-military shtick was really starting to get on Craig's wick.

"Anyway," Clive said, walking forward to put his right hand on Craig's left shoulder, "I think now's the time to muster some of that famous Tartan spirit. 'Rally behind the piper' and all that."

Margaret immediately stood back up supportively, as if stirred into action by Clive's call-to-arms.

"So," Clive continued, flashing Margaret a wink, "what we have here, in military parlance, in a right royal balls-up. British Tommy takes a wrong turn and is ambushed by circumstances. Backs to the wall. Bluff Cove, 1982. Special Ops." Craig noticed how much the old duffer seemed to be enjoying himself.

"Clive used to be in the SAS," Margaret explained. "He knows, well, you know, stuff."

Clive dropped his volume level conspiratorially.

"We only want to try and help, Craig. This is a serious situation and my experience could provide a path to safety." His initial bluster seemed, thankfully, have burnt itself out.

SUNSET OVER SUNSET © Steve Richards

"Trust me, son, there's always a way out of a situation. We just need to think of it. And not make one more false step or things could get quite...," he searched for the word, "...sticky."

Craig dropped his head slowly.

"Come on, love" said Margaret. "Let's have another drop of tea and break out the Tunnock's. I found somewhere down here that sells them. That's something, at least?" She also dropped her head in similar fashion and screwed up her eyes.

Clive Hackforth knew he was going to need to summon all of his old powers of motivation if he was going to rally these sorry troops.

"Fear not!" The volume was back up. "From what you've told me, old boy," he patted Craig's shoulder sharply. "It's never over until the rotund female warbles, as we used to say. We just need something on which to build our counter-offensive. A little ray of sunshine in this squally shower..."

"Well," said Craig, lifting his head. "I might have something to go on."

Clive straightened his back.

"I have stashed the murder weapon in the one place they'd never look," offered Craig, "under dad's commemoration stone at the crematorium. I was going to ditch it in the river but then thought it might come in useful later if they were able to tie it to the person who actually committed the killings."

"Well done, love," said Margaret. "Your dad would be proud of you."

"Nice of you to say so, mum. But if dad was here now, you and I both know he'd be doing his pieces."

SUNSET OVER SUNSET © Steve Richards

22
Nick of Time

Nick Sands had never really showed much discernible talent at anything before he joined the police force. He had always been a slightly awkward kid. 'Socially inept' was how one of his teachers had described him to his parents. His parents had always been very supportive, but Sands knew he wasn't cut out for a conventional future.

He struggled to make friends. He struggled to meet and impress girls. The strange thing was that he was never picked upon because he always seemed to exude an inner confidence that confused the bullies. Teachers often mistook it as arrogance.

He had sailed through exams. He was interested in the sciences rather than the arts and he knew he wasn't going to win any awards for oratory or joke-telling. His main strength was an all-seeing eye for detail. Not just being able to spot a typo from thirty feet, Sands' powers of observation were on another level.

From a young age, he noticed the little things others missed, whether it was the chewing gum the teenager was sticking to the underside of a restaurant table or the face a cheeky kid made behind his aunt's back. Sands didn't initially regard his strength as much of a strength at all. He thought everyone noticed the same things. They seemed glaringly obvious. But if 'Spot the Difference' pictures had been a competitive event, Sands would have been World and Olympic champion at the age of seven.

At college, Sands signed up for a chemistry degree. Under 'Observations' when writing up an experiment, while his peers scratched their heads, he simply wouldn't know where to start. But he knew he didn't want to be a chemist. He didn't want to spend his professional life stating what appeared to him to be the bleeding obvious. So it wasn't until one weekend in his final year when he visited a friend that his future career presented itself.

As it turned out, Sands wasn't the only natural introvert on his corridor in his Hall of Residence. There was a maths undergraduate nicknamed 'Wookiee' after Chewbacca from Star Wars because of his long hair and unkempt facial foliage.

Wookiee also had thick unfashionable glasses which made him 'the single most unattractive man in Western Europe' according to the resident wag. One Friday, Sands and Wookiee were the only people on the corridor to shun the visceral appeal of a live performance by *'Dumpy's Rusty Nuts'* at the Students' Union.

Sands was restless and noticed some guitar music coming from 'Wookiee's Lair', as it had been coined. He wandered up the corridor, stopped outside the hirsute lad's door and realised the guitar was being played live by someone inside.

He wondered if Wookiee had a visitor. The vision of a long-haired maths genius in bottle-top glasses, a white shirt and uncool jeans strumming out these infinitely cool licks didn't compute. Sands' light knock on the door was enough to silence the unseen guitar. He knocked again, adding the reassurance that it was 'only Nick, from along the corridor'.

A frantic scrape of chair-legs, a shuffle of feet, a clatter and a muffled expletive later and a crack in the door opened. Wookiee peered through and stared at his visitor.

"What do you want?" he said impassively.

"Have you got Keith Richards in there, Wookiee?"

"Eh?"

"Or maybe the reports of Jimi Hendrix's demise are somewhat premature." Sands added a wry, sympathetic smile to encourage Wookiee to play along.

Wookiee went to close the door.

"Wait!" Sands countered. "Just answer me this: Does our very own resident Chewbacca have a hidden talent as a rock god?"

SUNSET OVER SUNSET © Steve Richards

"Didn't have you down as one of the piss-take brigade," Wookiee said in a deadpan West Midlands drawl, peering again through a slightly wider crack in the door.

"It sounds great, Wookster," said Sands, "can I see the guitar?"

Wookiee looked suspiciously beyond Sands into the corridor. On confirmation that no one was lurking, he ushered his visitor into the room and proceeded to talk knowledgably and eloquently about his true passion for prog rock and its pantheon of great guitarists. Sands indulged him, such was the depth of his host's passion and enthusiasm. Having sworn an oath to conceal his new pal's secret from the 'poncy schoolboys' who lived elsewhere on the corridor, Wookiee and Sands fostered an unlikely friendship.

One weekend Wookiee announced to Nick that it was his 21st birthday and he wanted to invite his only friend to accompany him on a visit home. Sands couldn't think of an excuse quickly enough so the two of them caught the train to Wolverhampton and were picked up by Wookiee's mousy mother in an ancient chocolate brown Austin Allegro. Sands spent the car journey vowing to memorise an excuse he could trot out to avoid such traps in the future.

On the Saturday night, however, the burden was lifted considerably by the addition of Wookiee's dad. The three of them walked to a local pub to chew their way through some real ale and Sands found Wookiee's dad, Terry, a captivating character, full of charisma and interesting stories from his 20 years in the police force.

These were not bawdy stories of lasciviousness or violent encounters with unlikely ne'er-do-wells. They were detailed tales of how ingenuity and lateral thinking had cracked various cases. Suddenly, in Sands' eyes, there was an obvious and apparent value in possessing a rarely observant nature. And it came packaged within colourful stories stacked with roguery, jiggery-pokery and downright devilment.

Sands was hooked.

There was a live band on at the local and to commemorate his son's 21st, Terry had arranged a surprise. As the band finished a decent rendition of a Black Sabbath standard, the lead singer invited the birthday boy up to the stage to jam with them on their next track, a 12-minuute montage of Eric Clapton hits. His dad had even gone to the trouble of arranging for Wookiee's beloved Fender guitar to be picked up from his room back at University and transported to the gig.

After some initial reticence, broken down in part by the five pints of *Scrubster's Old Ballbreaker*, Wookiee joined the band and proceeded to play the rest of the musicians off the stage. At one point, the rest of them stopped altogether and Wookiee, long hair obscuring his face, was lost in a prolonged guitar solo that enraptured all 62 people in the audience, even down to the one-eyed bulldog that had been asleep under the next table until then.

Sands returned to college on the Sunday evening a changed man. He had learned some valuable lessons. The first was never to pigeon-hole people without getting to know them. The second was never, under any circumstances, to drink multiple pints of warm, flat ale at 6.5%. And the last was to enrol in the police force as soon as he graduated.

Back in the present, Sands' mobile rang. Randwick's name appeared on the handset.

"What's up?" Sands asked urgently, sat back in the main office with the HR people who were taking care of the paperwork now he had decided to end his extended break.

"Russian," came the reply, "similar M.O. to a couple of other recent murders. The victim has an arterial puncture in the neck. Left for dead but an ambulance happened to be on its way back from a false alarm and was just around the corner. Two minutes more and the man would've bled to death but they've managed to keep him alive for now. Just. Tough buggers, these Russians."

"Where?" Sands said, a staccato functionality coming back to him naturally after so many months of stagnation.

"St Thomas's," Randwick replied, "Intensive care. He's having blood transfusions but we need to be there the second he wakes up in case he doesn't make it."

"Twenty minutes," Sands said and immediately hung up.

23
Finding the Four Corners

Pieter covered Destiny's duties and clocked in the girls as they started to arrive at The Sunset early on Thursday evening. There was still no sign of the woman herself.

Seamus arrived back. He seemed agitated and hurried across the main floor to his office. Pieter tried to catch his eye to flag up Destiny's absence but to no avail. Pieter double-checked the staff rota to see if she had happened to have booked an impromptu day off but there was nothing marked.

A few customers had started to arrive. The main shows wouldn't start for a few hours but some regulars sometimes used the club to meet and discuss sensitive topics of conversation hidden from everyday punters in the local boozers. Two of today's customers, however, seemed to Pieter's experienced eye to be out of place.

One guy, in his mid-thirties was accompanied by what appeared to be his father. It could be an old-Queen-and-rent-boy combo, Pieter thought. Something about them didn't seem to fit, though.

They seemed to be having a good look around, taking it in turns to pretend to look for the Gents toilet. Surely one would tip off the other if they genuinely needed a piss. The older gent was well dressed in a grey suit and silk handkerchief. He repeatedly stroked his impeccably maintained grey moustache, exhibiting a degree of nervousness. The younger man also looked anxious and uncomfortable. If it was a father and son who'd stumbled across the club inadvertently, why had they paid the £10 entrance fee?

Pieter noticed that the younger man had already knocked back his pint so he wandered over to collect his glass.

"Good evening, gentlemen," Pieter said nonchalantly. "Are you here for the dancing later?"

SUNSET OVER SUNSET © Steve Richards

The older man was quick to take the lead. "Absolutely," he said with a comedic, upper-class twang. "What time do your bevvy of beauties strut their stuff?"

Pieter noticed he had a twinkle in his eye. His moustache twitched. Pieter immediately changed his assessment to a son taking his old dad out for a saucy treat on his birthday.

"I'm looking for a friend of mine," blurted out the younger man. He was sweating profusely.

"I doubt you'll find him in here," Pieter said, picking up the empty glass. "Get you another?"

Before Craig could answer, Clive stepped in. "I say," he said urgently, "we really are here looking for a young female friend of ours and I wondered if you might have seen her?" Pieter's attention was suddenly piqued.

"She's called 'Destiny,'" Craig added. Pieter visibly jumped. He stared back at each of the men in turn. He narrowed his gaze and leaned in conspiratorially.

"What do you know about D?" He looked around behind him quickly to see if anyone was watching. He then perched on a stool opposite them. "Where is she?"

Again, Clive took the lead. "Well, old fruit, I, er, well, er, we were wondering if you happened to know if she had any enemies?"

Pieter stared at him. "Enemies?" he replied, surprised. "Destiny is probably the sweetest, nicest, good-natured person I know." He looked at the younger man who had now dropped his head and was examining his footwear. "Now what the fuck is this all about?"

Across the club, Seamus had emerged from his office and was perusing his surroundings, looking for Pieter, who had his back to him, hunched forward and talking to what looked like an old dandy and a rent boy. They seemed to be talking intently. Seamus retreated into his office.

"It's probably nothing, old boy," Clive defused, holding up his right hand

SUNSET OVER SUNSET © Steve Richards

to pacify the man with the Eastern European accent. "It's just that, well, she's kind of gone missing."

Pieter straightened his back. "Yes," he said, "she hasn't shown up for work, which is very unlike her."

Clive continued. "So, and please forgive me for repeating myself," he was smiling deferentially, "but we were wondering if you might know if she was in any trouble, to your knowledge?" Pieter had been trained to refer anyone who turned up asking questions directly to Seamus.

"Right, let me stop you there," Pieter countered. "Firstly, I need you to tell me exactly who you are. And I want a straight answer."

The younger man, who wasn't enjoying any of this, muttered, "We're just friends of hers."

"Friends," Pieter said sarcastically. "Well, I've known Destiny for several years and I don't remember her ever mentioning you two lover-boys." Craig and Clive looked at each other. The latter spluttered, "Well, hold on just a...."

"Shut," Pieter pounced holding up his index finger, "the fuck up. I want you to simply answer my questions or I'm going to need you to talk to my boss and that is very likely to end badly for you."

Clive gestured that he was using an imaginary zip to close his mouth.

"Here's what we have here," Pieter summed up. "You two come here asking about a very good friend of mine who you say has gone missing. You say you know her but she has never mentioned you. You won't tell me who you are. You start talking about 'enemies'. My question, and it's a very simple one," the finger was raised again, "who are you and why are you here?"

Clive again jumped in. "Well, that's two questions, really, old stick..." Pieter's finger shot up. His stare bore into Clive.

Craig's turn. "All you need to know is that we are friends of Destiny. We know she works here. She is not returning our calls. We are simply trying

SUNSET OVER SUNSET © Steve Richards

to find out what might have happened to her."

"And that's it?" Pieter said. "Your friend doesn't return your call so you come to her work and start asking about enemies. This is bullshit. I think I need to get Seamus involved," Pieter added, standing up.

Clive started to stand up, "Come on, Craig, I think this man isn't going to help us," He was flustered.

At Pieter's shoulder, a new man joined the conversation. It was the man Clive had noticed watching them earlier from across the room.

"Problem, Pieter?" the man said congenially with an Irish lilt, choosing to fix his gaze on the younger man.

"No, Seamus," Pieter opined, "These two gentlemen were just leaving."

"Ah, such a shame," Seamus said, putting his hand on the older man's shoulder. Clive didn't like being touched. He immediately bristled and Craig thought a fight might break out, a fight that he and his septuagenarian tag-team partner would lose.

Again, Craig tried to defuse the situation. "Look," he said wearily, "it's nothing. We were just trying to find out some clue as to what might've happened to a friend of mine, that's all. It was a big waste of time, that's all. Now we're leaving."

"Which friend?" Seamus said casually.

Craig froze. He looked at the Irish man and every instinct he had told him to take flight. This had been a mistake. He needed to get himself and Clive out of there now.

Craig ushered Clive towards the exit. "Thanks again," he managed as they walked hurriedly down the stairs and into the street. Craig bent forward and put his hands on his knees. He thought he was going to be sick.

Back upstairs, it was Seamus's turn to be inquisitor.

SUNSET OVER SUNSET © Steve Richards

"What was all that about?" he asked Pieter, who was staring intently at his boss. Pieter paused, trying to read Seamus's expression.

"Er, nothing much," he lied. "Just two out-of-towners lost and confused in the big city." He hurried away back to the bar with the empty glasses.

SUNSET OVER SUNSET © Steve Richards

24
Bloody. Hell.

Shortly after Sands arrived at the hospital to question the Russian, his colleague's mobile started to ring. Randwick answered and listened intently, looking straight at Nick while he processed the information. Sands could tell it was not good news.

"22 Belsize Mansions, yes, I know it. Near the *Crown & Sceptre*, right?" He started to walk out of the ward, motioning Sands to follow him. "Basement flat. Right. Got it." The Russian would have to wait.

When they arrived, the whole street had been cordoned off with police tape. Randwick and Sands lowered their heads as they ducked under the tape, walking quickly towards the crime scene. Another member from the CID team, Dave Rushton, was waiting for them at one of the front doors of a smart terraced façade.

"Two vics," Rushton said, foregoing any pleasantries, leading the investigators into the building, talking over his shoulder as he went.

"One IC1 female, 20s and one IC3 male, early 30s. Both in states of undress, both with puncture wounds in the back. Both bled out. Or that's what it looks like."

"Thanks, Dave," Randwick said. "Anything else?"

"There's a lot of claret, Sarge," he added, stopping outside the interior floor of the basement flat. "And the dead bird's got a great rack." Sands hadn't missed Rushton's bathetic brand of humour during his absence.

Randwick and Sands opened the door and walked along the corridor towards their colleagues at the back of the flat. A photographer from the forensics team, dressed in a white boiler suit complete with white face mask, was taking photos of the deceased. Another man, similarly dressed, was taking a close look at the bodies. It was a man Randwick had worked with for years, a trusted and reliable man called Gethin

Davies whose strong Birmingham accent belied his Welsh moniker.

"Alright, John," Davies drawled to Randwiick. He ignored Sands.

"What've you got?"

"Two single puncture wounds on each vic. Both stabbed in the back by what looks to be the same weapon. Time of death looks like about 15 hours ago, give or take."

Randwick and Sands had both donned blue plastic overshoes and Sands was carefully treading around the bodies. Crime scenes always appealed to Sands' observant nature. In another life, he would've liked Davies' job.

The extent of the blood pool around each body had been marked out. Combined, they covered the majority of the floor so it was tricky to tip-toe a path to the female corpse, splayed face-down on the couch.

"Anything else yet?" Randwick asked.

"The perp' obviously knew what he was doing," Davies said. "The puncture wounds both entered the torso at the exact place to sever the hepatic portal vein. Tricky wire to cut if you're wildly slashing away. Both vics would've bled out quite quickly, lost consciousness within less than a minute. No visible signs of a major struggle. Fatal wounds look like they were delivered by someone's left hand."

Randwick perused the scene from the doorway. With four bodies in the small lounge, two of them still alive, space was at a premium. "First impressions, Nick? Boyfriend catches the female at it with Mr Gigolo, here, and offs them both?"

Sands directed his reply to Davies, while bending down to study the gold crucifix around the next of the black man. "Anything else at all, Gethin?"

"Well," the boiler-suited man said as he pressed the fingers of the woman's lifeless hand onto strips of sticky plastic. "There is one more thing..."

"Ok, Columbo," chipped in Randwick with half a smirk, "out with it."

SUNSET OVER SUNSET © Steve Richards

Without looking away from his task, Davies waved his left arm to towards the corner of the room to Randwick's left. "Well it's a quite a strange one really and one of the more sinister crimes I've seen in a while," he said, pausing as he lifted the fingers from the plastic and from his bent-forward position, looked up at Randwick.

"It looks like one of our victims here actually bought a Kula Shaker album. Criminal."

Sands ignored the quip, still inspecting the dead man's torso. "Looks like a print or something on this crucifix."

"Yeah, you see that sometimes with stab victims," Davies said. "People realise they're going to die and spend their final seconds holding their crucifix or lifting it to kiss it. 'Jesus Saves' and all that. Christ must've been having a fag-break when this poor bugger sought divine intervention."

"Do what you can, Gethin," Randwick told Davies. "These are two of a number of similar M.O.s we are investigating at present."

"It's just so neat and tidy," Sands said quietly, deep in thought.

"What do you mean?" asked Randwick.

"Just, so, well, *surgical*."

"No sign of a struggle," agreed Randwick, "and no real sign of defensive wounds on the vics."

"No, they knew their attacker alright," Davies chipped in.

"'Attacker', singular?" asked Randwick.

"Yeah, I think it's a single attacker, acting alone," Sands assessed, now staring intently at the two glasses on the table and stooping over to sniff at the contents. "No forced entry so they knew him. No major disturbance in here so they weren't expecting it. No reports from neighbours of shouting late at night."

Sands stood upright. "Gethin, can we get a hurry-up on toxicology for these two? Check it was them who were both drinking the ouzo and no-one else, he gestured towards the glasses.

He looked at Randwick then at the coffee-table book. "And if I'm not mistaken, this is our IC1 female on the front cover. Looks relatively recent so we should contact the photographer."

Randwick gave a hint of a wry smile. Sands had lost none of his bloodhound instincts despite his lay-off. Dave Rushden had followed along the corridor and stood behind Randwick.

"Flat belongs to a 'Claire Jones'. Matches the ID of our fallen maiden," he nodded past Randwick's shoulder towards the couch, "with the dynamite tits." Randwick rolled his eyes.

Rushton continued, "Neighbours reckon she works locally as a stripper or 'exotic dancer' as they put it. She went out late and doesn't usually arrive home 'til the wee small hours. They're not sure where she works but we're checking. Been here a couple of years. No steady boy- or girl-friend as far as they knew."

"Right you are, Dave," said Randwick. He turned back towards the murder scene to see Sands bending over the woman's back, looking intently at the puncture wound. Randwick thought back to his colleague's brush with death all those months ago. He knew his colleague was checking for similarities. Uncomfortable at the thought, Randwick said, "Right, Nick, shall we..?"

Sands looked to be lost in thought, peering into the puncture wound with his nose almost touching the corpse's flesh. Randwick looked at Davies who gave him a raised-eyebrows shrug.

"Nick," said Randwick more urgently, loud enough to shake Sands from his inspection. "Let's get moving. See if our Russian comrade at St Thomas's fancies giving us the benefit of his experience."

Sands looked up at him. "John, I really think we're looking for a surgeon."

SUNSET OVER SUNSET © Steve Richards

25
Cavalry Calls

Outside The Sunset Club, having just been told that prolonging their visit would severely damage their health, Craig and Clive took stock. The events of the previous hours had started to catch up with Craig and a fresh wave of exhaustion washed over him. By contrast, Clive was buzzing, his mind racing.

"Can I borrow your personal telephone thingy, Craig?" he asked.

Craig wearily looked at him then fished his mobile out of his pocket. He flicked its start button. There was a text from Anita.

'Still alive? What's ur ETA tomorrow?'

No kiss, Craig noted. He didn't have the nerve or inclination to reply.

"Not much battery left." he said, passing his iPhone to Clive who took it hesitantly. "No expert on these contraptions, I'm afraid. Don't suppose you could enlighten me as to how to dial a number?"

Craig had his eyes closed, pinching the bridge of his nose with his thumb and index finger. A boomer of a headache was on the way. You tell me the number and I'll punch it in. Clive trotted it out and on taking the handset, started marching off quickly.

Craig sat on a low wall opposite The Sunset Club. He didn't know what to make of his mother's new beau. He wasn't sure of anything. He wanted to climb into bed, disappear under the duvet and never emerge again.

Clive was talking intently into the handset but using it more like a walkie-talkie than a phone, holding it in front of his mouth to speak, then holding it up to his ear for the reply. Craig numbly wondered if he was suffixing every one of his verbal volleys with the word 'over'.

Earlier that day, in the upstairs office of The Sunset, another intense conversation had taken place. Seamus Twite was rattled. It happened rarely, but when it did, he sought support from the man who had stuck by him resolutely over the years, his elder brother, Shaun.

Shaun had always been protective towards Seamus. As they grew up in Newry, near the Southern Irish border, Shaun had been groomed for a leading role in the paramilitary organisation in which their father had been an active member since the fifties. The 1970s and '80s had been a tough environment for Seamus. Not blessed, or encumbered depending on how you think about it, with his brother's physical menace, Seamus had concentrated on the power of his words and intelligence to earn respect. But he had been unable to assert influence and garner respect befitting of his ambition.

There always seemed to Seamus to be so many people involved in the decisions. Also, seniority seemed to be dictated by age rather than ability and as the youngest of four brothers, Seamus's prospects of rising to be top dog fell somewhere between unlikely and non-existent.

Seamus's principal frustration, however, was the in-fighting between families who were nominally on the same side. As the 90s dawned, it was clear that the people at the top of the organisation were planning to do their fighting at the negotiating table. The thrill had gone out of it, the danger that had kept Seamus interested. In his teenage years, Seamus had also become disenchanted with the lack of financial reward that came with all of the risk. He had always had a taste for the finer things and loved the feeling of having a pocketful of cash when all around him had nothing. It seemed to add a couple of inches to his 5 foot 9 stature.

Branching out on his own was not an option while his father was still alive and Shaun was so involved. To distract himself, Seamus took to his books. Ever since he had dissected a toad in a biology lesson and inflated its lungs with a straw, Seamus had been fascinated by the processes that brought things to life not to mention those that took it away.

The fragility of life became apparent and it enraptured Seamus; a malfunction from just one small, seemingly insignificant cog in the engine could end it all. It mirrored his own plight on one level, he being the small, under-appreciated cog with the potential to turn everything to dust. Physiology seemed to make sense to him instinctively. He excelled in exams and he set himself a goal of becoming a surgeon.

One cold winter night, early on in his professional medical training, Shaun woke his brother and hurriedly dragged him downstairs.

Sat at the kitchen table was a man he had never seen but knew as 'Shug', a violent enforcer with a fearsome reputation. A paramilitary operation had gone awry and Shug had become isolated, pinned down in a gun battle and captured. He had then been thrown out of a moving car outside the Twite family home having had his left leg shattered by a gunshot to his kneecap.

He had lost a lot of blood and was fading in and out of consciousness. Shaun cleared the kitchen table and Seamus went to work. HIs brother watched him intently as he took time to wash his hands thoroughly and don his medical gloves before inspecting the wound impassively then tying off the relevant veins. Shaun was amazed and impressed by his brother's speedy efficiency. He seemed to know exactly what to do to stop the bleeding and reset the bones.

Having stitched up the wounds, he rigged a splint and then started to mix some plaster of Paris to make a cast. Seamus had played fast and loose with the college's rules around taking the hospital's medical materials home. Reports of his sterling performance quickly percolated throughout the organisation and several times subsequently he had been employed to patch up wounded men.

Having then graduated with flying colours, he got a highly paid job at a private clinic. He moved away and bought a flash car. But it was not enough. Seamus wanted more; to build his own organisation, not tied to any political mantra but for the express accumulation of wealth. Seamus knew that huge wealth meant significant power so to maximise his earnings he quit his career and moved to London, well away from his family's stifling spectre.

Seamus explained to his family that he had fallen out of love with surgery and he wanted to accelerate his career in the big city. The Troubles were long since over and he explained to his older brother that he missed the excitement of regaling against the system, of outsmarting the authorities against all odds. The brothers' father had since passed away and as the newly ensconced patriarch, Shaun had other fish to fry rather than worry about his materialistic, smart-arsed brother.

So after Seamus left, Shaun heard from a few old contacts that his wee brother had recruited a small number of ex-paramilitary contacts to work in 'security'. They were well trained, organised and above all, fiercely loyal. Seamus knew their past indiscretions made it difficult to walk into legal, gainful employment. These guys were all experienced pros. No silly mistakes. No histrionics. No fuss. Shaun knew his brother had left the medical profession and secretly wished him well but had not heard from him in over a year until now.

"Shaun," said Seamus.

"Long time," came the reply, low-pitched Northern Irish clipped accent.

"How's Ma?"

"She's fine. Seamus. What do you want?" Idle chit-chat didn't come easy to the Twite brothers.

"I might need some help, Shaun." said Seamus, cutting to the chase. "In the last wee while I've been building something over here. It has gone reasonably well. Doing ok. No ripples. But the competition is starting to throw its weight about and I might need a few of our old comrades to boost the ranks temporarily."

Seamus was trying desperately not to sound needy. He had been self-sufficient for years. Asking his older brother for help had always been a last resort. But Seamus felt something was brewing and he didn't want to be out-flanked or out-muscled.

There was a pause at the end of the line. Seamus pictured his brother's strong features across the Irish sea. He knew he would be stood in his kitchen, peering out of the window over the field.

"Seamus," he said eventually, "it's been a long time."

"I know, I should've been in touch sooner..."

SUNSET OVER SUNSET © Steve Richards

"No, it's not that," Shaun interrupted, irritation in his voice. "The reinforcements you're after have moved on. The ones who wanted to stay active are otherwise engaged. And the others are now out of practice. Some of the best are in their sixties now, Seamus, for fuck's sake..."

It was Seamus's turn to pause and think. Before he could reply, though, Shaun sighed then broke the silence.

"How many, where and when?"

Just as the smile spread across Seamus's face, in a different part of London another family gangland conversation was taking place, this time face-to-face. Donny Blanchard, head of the family firm sat opposite his son, Donald, across the pub-garden-style bench outside his mock Tudor mansion in Beckenham, just to the south east of London. Donald had been round for his dinner but when conversations of a sensitive nature took place, the father and son always retired to the well-tended patio that overlooked the lawns and rhododendrons.

"The thing is, son, we can't use the normal tactics with this fucker," said Donny, noticing two drops of recently dripped gravy on the front of his pink Ralph Lauren polo shirt. "He's different. No emotion. *Clinical*."

Donald was listening respectfully but his mind raced with murderous intent. Ever since the episode in Seamus's office, Donald had been dreaming up increasingly horrific ways for him to exact his revenge.

"But now that tart that worked for him is brown bread according to our man Rushton, so he might be shaken up a bit. Unless he did it himself, which he could've done, the sick bastard. Either way, son, he's ripe to make a mistake. So we need to be ready."

Donny rocked back as he blew a large plume of cigar smoke backwards. The bench creaked under his considerable frame. He was in his mid-fifties now, and was still a formidable physical presence heralding from a promising amateur boxing career.

Donald inspected his dad's growing paunch. He had followed his father down the amateur boxer path but he had maintained his fitness. He was a younger, leaner version of his father, twice as strong and twice as ambitious.

Donald was excited. He loved this kind of meeting with his dad. He had worked hard and it was gratifying now that he'd been invited into his dad's inner sanctum, where the big decisions were discussed and agreed. Donald's last meeting with the Irishman had been electrifying for all the wrong reasons. He was itching to move against him but he agreed with his dad - the Irishman was a worthy foe and they needed to be careful.

"Do you want me to call Kenny and get some of the boys up from Hastings?" Donald asked.

"Yes, son" Donny said, a proud glint in his eye. Donald's impulsiveness had got him into trouble many times, but his encounter with the Irishman had seemed to do him some good. Perhaps that chastening experience would be the making of him. In truth, Donny had been getting tired of all the recent hassle and he wondered when might be the right moment to pass the reins to his son.

The racketeering had become harder. No one respected the boundaries any more. The 'understandings' that had existed in the 70s and 80s, when there was enough to go round for all had been eroded. The Eastern Europeans had muscled in, the Jamaicans had become stronger, and now this new Irish fella was making life difficult and Donny was starting to wonder if he had the stomach for the fight.

Donald sensed his moment was close but he didn't want to push things too quickly with his father, who he had idolised for decades. Growing up as the eldest son of a villainous gangster had had its own benefits. He was never picked on at school, he always had plenty of cash to buy the best stuff and he'd even had his pick of the best looking girls, seduced by the trappings of wealth.

His dad had kept him shielded from the worst of the violence. He knew certain heads had been knocked together to retain order and maintain boundaries but Donny Blanchard had played his cards well over the years. He had built a valuable network of contacts in high places that

SUNSET OVER SUNSET © Steve Richards

came in useful if the finger was ever pointed towards him.

"It'll be ok, dad," Donald said as he watched his father chomping thoughtfully on his stogie.

"'Course it will, son," reassured Donny. He leaned forward and gripped his son's left hand with his huge right paw. "No one facks with the Blanchards. This Mick is going to find out all about it." He smiled broadly. "Now you call Kenny and get some of his best men drafted in. None of those young Asbo football hooligan hotheads. The proper boys, with the proper toys." Donald returned his dad's smile.

"How many, where and when?"

Twelve miles further north, a decorated Russian ex-serviceman marched into St Thomas's hospital. Flanked by two smaller, younger men, Dmitri Usanov was in no mood to be denied access to the comrade-in-arms who he had worked alongside for nearly twenty years. Sergei Ilic was like a younger brother and he had rarely been hurt.

Sergei was a man with expert skills borne from years of Special Forces training with the Russian military. He also had a sixth sense for anticipating danger and Dmitri realised that it would have taken a well-organised adversary to have out-flanked a man that was still a ball of muscle even though he was nearer 40 than 30.

Earlier that day Sergei had failed to meet Dmitri as arranged. He had not returned his call as protocol dictated and communications in and out of local hospitals had been tracked, revealing a chance pick-up by an ambulance crew on its way back from a false alarm following a tip-off.

The unconscious man had a neck wound and the ambulance men had found him gaffer-taped to a chair. Dmitri knew immediately it was Sergei. He should have accompanied his man on the mission but there seemed no reason to suspect there'd be a problem. And Sergei liked to work alone if at all possible. The crackling radio message reported that the man had lost a lot of blood but still had a pulse. If they had not happened to be nearby, the man would have been dead.

SUNSET OVER SUNSET © Steve Richards

The protruding vein at Dmitri's temple pulsed with rage. Their operation had been established for a decade in London. They had carved a niche to supply rich clients with drugs and girls - or occasionally boys. They worked this market and the other players largely left them alone, on the understanding that they kept to their niche.

Dmitri had heard that tensions were high among the other main gangs but their dealings had progressed undisturbed - until now. He knew that investigating officers would first go to the crime scene rather than the hospital. If he moved quickly he knew he might be able to get to Sergei and find out what had happened and who was about to feel the full force of the Russian's vengeance.

Dmitri signalled for the two henchmen to stay in the hospital's A & E area while he approached the desk.

"Hello," he said with a clipped Russian accent accompanied by the most disarming smile he could conjure. The charm offensive was on. Dmitri knew he was an intimidating physical presence at 6 feet 4 inches tall. He always dressed in black from head to toe which didn't do much to reinforce the avuncular tone he was trying to set with the young black nurse behind the reception desk.

"I am Dmitri," he added, "from Russia." The nurse gave him a thin, weary smile. He contorted his facial features to make his best 'anxiously pained' expression. The nurse thought he looked symptomatic of severe constipation.

"My brother, Sergei, was admitted recently to this hospital and it is imperative that I see him immediately." The nurse looked at him, unimpressed. His English was pretty good but laced with a very strong accent. With more urgency, desperately trying to keep his internal rage in check, Dmitri said, "I heard he has lost a lot of blood. He has a rare blood type. I am a direct match. He is my brother, you understand."

Again, not a flicker of interest or concern from the nurse. She had seen it all before. In a calm voice she replied, "I can assure you, 'Dmitri from Russia', that St Thomas's hospital is one of the best equipped hospitals in Britain, if not the world. If, indeed, your, er, 'brother' needs a transfusion, he will get what he needs. Now if I can take a few details..."

SUNSET OVER SUNSET © Steve Richards

She looked at her computer screen and tapped some keys. Dmitri had to use every last ounce of self-restraint to stop himself reaching across the desk and snapping the woman's slender neck. His window of opportunity was closing with every unproductive sentence.

In the waiting area, a drunk man with his arm in a makeshift sling was pulling faces at the two angular hard men sat opposite him. They stared at him without the merest hint of a facial flicker. They both glanced over periodically to see how their boss was getting on with the nurse. They realised too that the clock was ticking.

At that moment, Dmitri's emitted a loud, "Thank you kindly, madam" and pushed a flattened palm in their direction to indicate they should stay where they were. He turned his back and started along the corridor looking at the signs. He had apparently got what he wanted. The henchmen both knew he always did, in the end.

Dmitri then suddenly stopped and walked towards his men. The slightly larger henchman knew exactly what to ask as his boss bent down to converse.

The English equivalent of his question: "How many, where and when?"

At almost exactly the same time back in central London, opposite The Sunset Club another ex-serviceman, this one thirty years Dmitri's senior, was making a phone call on a borrowed mobile phone.

"Smudger. It's Clive." His tone was impatient and insistent. "Please don't talk, my dear old thing, I have some rather urgent instructions to impart. Is Marjorie in the same room?"

He listened and seemed pleased with the answer. He looked directly at Craig who was sat on a wall ten metres away.

"I have a young man who needs our help, Smudge," said Clive. "You see he's managed to get himself in one hell of a scrape. It's time to round up the troops for one last hurrah."

"Always a pleasure, Major" said the man on the other end of the line cheerfully. "Will be just like days of yore. How many, where and when?"

SUNSET OVER SUNSET © Steve Richards

26
Trouble & Strife

Craig watched Clive bark into his mobile and his thoughts turned to home.

He'd left less that 48 hours earlier and everything had been fine. Well, not fine, exactly. He was unfulfilled by his job. He was frustrated that his wife didn't share his immediate yearning for a family. And, if he laying all his cards on the table, he was niggled by Hibernian's continuing defensive lapses against the counter attack. All things considered though, the prospect of being incarcerated for double murder hadn't appeared in the itinerary for his latest trip.

He pictured the murder weapon he'd stashed under his father's internment stone. He pictured his father's face. Strong features, grey mane of hair, icy blue eyes. If he was here, he might know what to do. Craig had never missed him more than at this precise moment.

He was at a stage where he just wanted it to all be over. If he was to be arrested, fine. He didn't have the energy to resist. As Clive gave him back his phone, he knew he would have to call his wife. Anita deserved to know what was happening. He had already extended his stay in London for one extra night and there was no way he could jump on a flight and head for the hills. He knew he was still to respond to her earlier text.

In complete contrast to Craig's mental and physical state, Clive looked invigorated. He was stroking his moustache and seemed energised by his phone call. He indicated he was off to find a tobacconist to replenish his stock of slim panatela cigars which he referred to as 'cigarillos'. He told Craig to sit tight.

Craig pressed the touchscreen to bring up his wife's number. It was late-afternoon. She would probably be in a meeting. An image of her bouncy hair, petite frame and killer heels formed in Craig's mind. He imagined her busily and conscientiously going about her business. Driven and diligent. Focused. The antithesis of how he felt.

He paused then hit the number, pressed the phone to his ear and closed his eyes so he could concentrate. He had no idea what he was going to say.

She answered almost immediately with a brisk, "Hello, Craig." Her tone seemed calm, steady. Not as irritated as he expected. Craig thought the phoneline was amazingly clear. It was as though she was stood right in front of him in the flesh. He instinctively opened his eyes.

It was her. In the flesh. Stood directly in front of him.

Craig blinked in astonishment. She lowered his phone from his ear. "You need to let me know what's going on."

Craig couldn't quite understand what was happening. Was this some kind of hallucination? He had been under a lot of stress. Was this whole fucking mess some kind of sickeningly realistic dream? Oh, please let that be true.

Anita was disturbed by her husband's dishevelled and confused appearance. She took his phone from his hand as he gawped at her, disconnected and offered his phone back to him. She put her hand on his shoulder and bent towards him.

"Craig, it's me. I'm here." She could tell something was badly wrong. Craig silently stared at her.

"Let's go," she said, taking the lead. "I just walked past a cafe. It looked quiet, we can get a wee cuppa tea there. You look like you could do with it. I get the feeling I'm going to need one too."

She took his hand and led him away. He silently followed.

A few minutes later, they sat opposite each other in a booth in an independent Italian-run café, the kind of place where a double espresso would keep a man, on the verge of death, alive for another month. There was only one other table occupied. Two women looked like they had skived off work for coffee and cake.

Anita and Craig stared at each other. A cup of rooibos tea and a cappuccino sat between them.

SUNSET OVER SUNSET © Steve Richards

Gazing at their drinks, Craig said absent-mindedly, "If this was Italy they wouldn't probably serve you a cappuccino." Anita stared back. "It's afternoon," he explained, his voice drifting off,"...cappuccino's a morning drink in Italy..."

Anita was trying to weigh up if he was drunk or having a mental breakdown. Or both.

"How?" he asked, pathetically. "How did you find me?"

Anita took her own phone from her jacket pocket and shook it from side to side in front of his face. Craig noticed for the first time that she had a small overnight bag with her.

"'Find my iPhone,'" she said. Craig wrinkled his nose. "It's an app that tracks your phone using GPS."

"My phone?" he asked.

"Any phone." Her tone was calm and sympathetic. Craig still couldn't believe his wife was sat opposite him. He reached out to touch her arm, as if to make sure she was actually there.

She continued, "People use it to track their phone if it gets stolen. You can't turn the tracker off. Well, it's difficult anyway. I added your phone to the app. and my iPad lead me straight to you." He stared at her blankly. "I thought you might be in a meeting, not, well, just sat on a wall making a phone call..."

She looked down trying to find the right words. "Look, you know the last few months haven't been, well, great. I've been consumed by work and, well, I can understand it to some extent, but you've been, well, distant."

"Distant?" he repeated.

"Yes, distant. Well, what with you off to London every week, I had no idea where you were or what you might be getting up to so I thought it might be useful...you know...to know where you were..."

"Useful..." he said sarcastically.

SUNSET OVER SUNSET © Steve Richards

"You know, if I ever needed to contact you," Anita said, backtracking.

Craig said sourly, "You've been tracking me?" He was offended. "Like one of those ankle tags worn by criminals or...or one of those chipped dogs."

"Well, what if your phone had actually been stolen? You'd have thanked me!" she countered.

"You've been tracking me because you don't trust me, Anita. Plain and simple."

She bowed her head in accordance. He shook his head softly. "You've been tracking me because of what you think 'I get up to', as you so subtly just put it."

"I was worried, that's all," she said defensively. She looked at her husband and decided to rise above his accusations to tackle the situation at hand. "Craig," she said reaching out to hold both of his hands with hers, "tell me what has happened."

Craig stared back at her blankly. He genuinely didn't know where to start. Clive burst into the cafe and moved quickly towards Craig.

"There you are, old boy!" he expounded. "Thought I'd bloody well lost you! I thought I told you to stay put."

Clive turned to Anita then back to Craig.

"I say, you're a quick worker" he said. He reached out his right hand towards Anita and bowed.

"Clive Hackforth, DSC, retired. It's an absolute pleasure to make your acquaintance."

Anita glared at him then back at Craig who had put his head in his hands. "Clive," Craig said, "go and get yourself a nice frothy Italian coffee and come and join my wife and I in ten minutes." He finished the sentence by mimicking Clive's upper-class accent, adding, "There's a good chap."

Back at St Thomas's hospital, Dmitri had found the room where the medics had taken Sergei. Two uniformed police officers were posted outside. They had reacted quicker than he'd expected. He went to walk into the treatment room but he was rebuffed by both officers who stood up to block Dmitri's way.

"Ah, hello, officers," said Dmitri, the charm offensive back in full swing. "My brother has been injured and I need to see him immediately."

"No one in or out," enforced the slightly larger of the two policemen.

"Yes, I know, officer, but you don't understand. He has a rare blood type. I'm here to save his life."

"No one in or out" repeated the slightly smaller officer. Dmitri knew he could brush both men aside with ease if he wanted to but it would cause problems. He needed access to Sergei without causing alarm.

"I hope your conscience will cope with a possible death of a Russian national," glowered Dmitri, straightening his back to present his full height. Both policemen looked suitably intimidated but he couldn't afford to push his luck. He walked back down the corridor and turned a corner to take stock and think.

A doctor was coming towards him from the other direction, pre-occupied with the details on his clip-board. He almost bumped into the Russian. On glancing up at Dmitri's burly physique, the doctor began to splutter a profuse apology. Waving it away, Dmitri led the man by his elbow to the edge of the corridor and leaned closer to whisper in his ear.

"Hey, no problem, Doc. Listen, I wonder if you help a poor worried man find out what has happened to his dear brother."

The doctor looked up at his chiselled face, back down to his clipboard and then started to mumble an excuse. As he started to move away, Dmitri tightened the grip on his elbow. The doctor flinched. Dmitri leaned in again, conspiratorially, "Look, Doctor, I'm sure you probably have a brother or sister?" Without waiting for an answer, he continued, "My only brother was brought here in the last hour and there are two officers on the door who won't let me see him. Someone has hurt him pretty

SUNSET OVER SUNSET © Steve Richards

bad. I need to know who it was."

The doctor stared into the Russian's eyes and detected genuine concern.

"Don't you want to find out what happened to him first rather than who did it?"

Dmitri back-tracked, "Of course, doctor, of course I want to know his condition. It is my bad English," he added with an extra dollop of Russian accent.

The doctor looked past the man's shoulder as if trying to find someone to help him break out of the uncomfortable tete-a-tete. No one.

He looked up at Dmitri, "Look, this is very irregular." Dmitri leaned in slightly closer. "But I was the attending doctor who treated your brother. I'm sorry to report that he's in very bad shape. He almost bled to death."

Dmitri listened, transfixed. The doctor noticed the Russian's jaw muscle twitch as he imparted the news. "An artery in his neck has been severed. Another three minutes and your brother would've died."

"But who did this thing?" Dmitri's patience was wearing thin.

"I'm afraid I have no idea," the doctor said, holding up a hand as if to pacify his audience. Dmitri tightened the grip on his elbow hard enough to stop the circulation. The doctor winced uncomfortably. Still no-one came down the corridor to intervene.

"Look," the doctor said reluctantly, "all I know is what I overheard from those two policemen." The Russian's eyes widened.

The doctor paused again. "I really shouldn't be providing information...." Dmitri furrowed his brow with just enough menace to get the man to finish his sentence "...but apparently they almost apprehended the suspects, a gang of six men. They mentioned a name..." he tapped his clipboard with the tip of his pen as if to aid his memory "...Danny Blanchflower...Danny Blanchings...?"

"Donny Blanchard," Dmitri mumbled, instantly releasing the man to

SUNSET OVER SUNSET © Steve Richards

stride back down the corridor towards the waiting room.

Behind him, the doctor sprang forward and pushed open a store room five metres ahead of him on the left of the corridor. Once inside he pulled out a mobile phone and took off his white coat, hanging it onto a hook on the back of the door. He threw his clipboard onto a chair. The number connected.

"Ah, Donny. It's your favourite bog-trotter here." There was a pause as Seamus listened to the response.

"Woa, woa, Donny, that's *Mister* 'Irish Prick' to you." Seamus listened, a smile under his nose. He held the phone slightly away from his ear to distance himself from the stream of abuse being emitted.

"I tell ya what, Donny," Seamus interrupted, "you Londoners love a swear word, so you do."

He listened for a few seconds then interrupted again, raising his voice and holding the door closed with his shoulder.

"Well, if you'd shut your foul mouth for a second, I'm actually phoning you with some useful information. My network of connections has brought it to my attention that Dmitri and his Russian crew are on their way to pay you a visit. And it's not to deliver some of those Russian dolls that are so full of themselves.

"They are particularly upset, by all accounts. Something about you trying to assassinate one of their main men. So, all I'm saying, Donny, old boy, is that I'd make sure I was prepared for a Red Dawn. These Commies don't fuck about." Seamus listened for a few seconds at another barrage of verbal vitriol then chipped back in.

"And just one thing before I go, Donny," said Seamus. "It's about the bad language." He held the phone closer to his mouth to increase his volume without raising his voice.

"If you want a swear-off, cunty-bollocks, you picked the wrong nationality. Oh, fuck-a-doodle-doo, yes, Donny. The Irish invented fucking swearing and if you want to cunt the fuck out of it, shite-units like you should

SUNSET OVER SUNSET © Steve Richards

realise when they're out of their twatting depth."

Donny was obviously trying to butt in, so Seamus raised his voice and leaned harder into the door.

"Shut your facial hole, ya Pearly Cock-and-balls. If you'd shut the twat up for two secs, you'd take my cunting advice, ya bell-sucking khazi-licking rancid bucket of whore-cum. If Dmitri doesn't slit your putrid gizzard, tossy-tits, I'll ram a Bowie knife so far up your shitter it'll take yer fucking tonsils out."

He disconnected before Donny could reply, opened the door and walked confidently down the corridor, a steely look in his eye. As he reached the waiting room, he walked over to the black nurse on reception and surreptitiously passed her a small wedge of folded £50 notes.

"Perfection, Gabby. Perfection." he said under his breath before marching over to the public phone attached to the wall. He then fished out his mobile to look up a number which he typed into the payphone.

"Soho CID, please," he said.

After a few seconds, he added, "Yes, can you please pass on a very important message to Detective Sergeant John Randwick. Do you have a pen? Yep, ok. Right, make sure you tell him that the Russians are on the move to take out Donny Blanchard. Yep, Blan-chard" He spelled out the name.

"There's gonna be a war at Blanchard's lock-up in New Cross."

Seamus replaced the receiver and strutted towards the exit, unable to keep the smile from his lips.

SUNSET OVER SUNSET © Steve Richards

27
Rope Ladder

A mile or two further North, Clive was sheepishly approaching Craig and Anita. He had some information to impart but the couple weren't exactly painting a picture of marital bliss as they sat opposite each other in the Italian cafe near The Sunset Club.

"Look," Clive said, as he shimmied himself into the table's fixed seats, next to Anita and diagonally opposite Craig, "I know you two might have all the harmony of Galtieri and Thatcher discussing the Malvinas in '82, but we have a situation here and I think I might have an idea."

"I was afraid you might say that," said Craig laconically.

Anita looked at Clive. "You know that we appreciate your help, Clive. It's just that I think the best option here – in fact the *only* sensible option - is to contact the police. I know Craig should've done it yesterday morning, but, well, what's done is done. Tell the truth and they'll understand. They'll work out what really happened and they'll let him go and we can get back to normal."

"It's too late for that, Anita, I've just told you," said Craig, shaking his head sorrowfully. "My DNA was at the murder scene. I'm probably on every CCTV camera in Soho following her home. She contacted me on Facebook that same morning. I left the flat without calling the police. The murder weapon has my fingerprints all over it." He looked at Clive then back to his wife. "I'm 'Donald Ducked.'"

"Well," said Clive, his moustache twitching furtively, "I'd agree that you've probably had finer hours, young man, but all might not be lost." Anita raised her eyebrows to encourage him to continue.

"You remember earlier, Craig," Clive continued, "when we went into The Sunset Club?"

"Feels like a lifetime ago…"

SUNSET OVER SUNSET © Steve Richards

"Well," Clive said, "you probably didn't notice but there was a job advert on the wall, near the entrance." He paused, looked at Craig who had his head bowed, then looked at Anita. "It was for a dancer."

"Sorry to break it to you, Clive" Craig said, still perusing his crotch, "but you've not got the legs for it."

"But you have, my dear," Clive said to Anita. "You see, if we're to get to the bottom of this whole rather unfortunate escapade, it would really help to have someone, well, *on the inside*."

Craig was irritated. "This 'escapade', Clive, in case you hadn't noticed, isn't a fucking game show. This is my fucking life. Right here and now." Anita looked around appalled at Craig's language. She hunched her shoulders and Craig lowered his voice accordingly as he continued.

"This 'unfortunate' set of circumstances might well royally fuck me up. I think it might be an idea to keep Anita out of the whole sorry fucking mess, don't you…old bean?"

Clive looked shocked and crestfallen by the machine gun burst of expletives. Anita stepped in.

"Look, Craig," she said in her most business-like tone, "I've come slightly late to this party so please excuse me if I'm missing something important, but things aren't looking especially rosy as far as I can make out. Options would appear to be limited, and, yes, there's a better than average chance you might be, as you perhaps should've put it, *compromised*."

She squeezed her husband's hand and turned to Clive. "So if getting a job in that cess-pit over the road might give us an edge, I might be up for doing it but I'm going to need to understand what the end game is."

Craig looked appalled. Clive looked like he was in love.

She continued, "Let's look at what we know. Firstly, that this old *girlfriend* of yours," she held up a finger to silence Craig's protest at the 'g' word, "okay, 'friend from Uni' was working at the Club before she was killed. What else do we know?"

SUNSET OVER SUNSET © Steve Richards

Craig jumped in, stimulated by Anita's drive. "Well, we know that the bar manager bloke, you know, the Eastern European bloke, knows we weren't there for a quiet drink. We also know that the club owner guy who came over to us at the end is dodgy. He looked like a nasty bastard."

Clive's turn. "And we also know that they know more than they're letting on. Thirty years' experience in Covert Ops tells me that."

"But who is the black guy in the girl's flat?" said Anita. Craig noticed she avoided using her name. "And why would someone want her dead? Want both of them dead?"

Clive chipped in, "The police will be catching up by now. I expect they'll be all over the Club soon, almost as soon as they find the bodies. They might've already been, which would explain the guys' jumpiness at the Club. So whatever plan we hatch, we'll need to be discreet."

"I'm not getting you involved," Craig said to Anita, belatedly returning the hand-squeeze.

"But that's just it, Craig," she said. "I *am* involved. My husband is going to be prime suspect for a double murder. If you're convicted, *my* marriage is over too. No prospect of any little Craigs and Anitas down the road." Craig stared at her.

"That's part of the reason I came down here, Craig. To tell you I think I'm ready."

"Bravo!" exclaimed Clive, patting Anita rather hard on the back.

Clive looked at Craig who had started to well up.

"Righto," Clive said, seizing the initiative, full of zest and conviction, "about that plan..."

SUNSET OVER SUNSET © Steve Richards

28
The Missing Link

Randwick listened intently to the message being relayed via his phone. Sands studied his boss's face, looking for clues of what was being said. Again, it didn't look like a call trumpeting good news about a win on the Premium Bonds. Randwick disconnected.

"Right, Nick, we need to get back to St. Thomas's. The stab victim's a Russian. Looks like it could be our surgeon friend's handiwork."

They sped across Westminster Bridge, sirens blaring from their unmarked police car. It was getting dark and the relentless London traffic impeded their progress. Pulling up outside, they hurried in, pushing past a guy that Sands noticed had a strange smirk on his face.

They hurried via the reception desk to meet two officers stationed outside the victim's room. Randwick had made sure the man was guarded the second he arrived. He couldn't afford for someone to pop by and finish what they'd started.

"All quiet?" he asked, as he flashed his ID to the attending officers.

"Kind of," said the taller one.

"What do you mean?" Randwick said, the stress starting to darken his mood. Things seemed to be spiralling out of control. He needed straight, efficient answers from those around him.

"Well," said the shorter officer, "we got door-stepped by some big ugly Russian wanting to give his brother in there a blood transfusion."

"Older guy with a face like granite?" Sands asked.

Both officers nodded.

"Dmitri," Sands said softly to Randwick.

"Let's go and see what his comrade-in-arms has to say, then," said Randwick, pushing open the doors. His phone started to ring in his pocket.

"Randwick," he answered.

He stopped dead when the message started to be relayed. He looked at Sands. Again, it appeared to be troublesome tidings. He pushed the button to disconnect and looked at Sands in exasperation before starting to move back towards the A&E.

"Tip off. Decent source. The Russians are moving against the Blanchards. New Cross. It's happening, Nick. Right now. It's gonna get choppy. Armed units have been alerted."

Sands wondered if the space-time continuum had realigned in the months he'd been away because things seemed to be moving ridiculously and unsettlingly fast since his return to duty. As if to emphasise the point, his own phone rang. He could see from the display that the call was from forensics division. He was following Randwick at a canter as he spoke, racing back to the squad car.

"Gethin, it's Nick. What have you got?"

Gethin Davies's unmistakeable Brummie accent bleated down the phone "It's the two vics from earlier with rear ventilation."

"Yes, yes," Sands said. He was starting to get short of breath. All of those months sat around his flat had done little for his fitness level.

"Something weird came up so I thought I'd give you a bell as soon as."

"Yes..." prompted Sands.

"We found some hairs on the pillow of the spare room. And we also found a small amount of semen on the side of the sink in the bathroom. The DNA from both samples match."

"But there was no sexual assault you seemed to think initially, at the murder scene" puffed Nick.

SUNSET OVER SUNSET © Steve Richards

"No," drawled Davies, "there wasn't."

"So…" Sands had reached the car and clambered into the passenger seat. Randwick had already pulled away before Sands had fully shut the door. The car lurched and Sands shot forward, banging the elbow holding the phone into the dashboard.

"Soooo…" Davies mimicked, "it looks like there was a third person staying in that flat last night. But he has scarpered. We ran a trace but no hits on the database. But if you get a suspect in custody, it's gonna take some explaining if we get a DNA match to the flat, wouldn't you say…?"

"Could be a flat-mate," Sands said, scrambling to click shut his seatbelt. They were zooming South, sirens wailing.

"Could be David Bloomin' Beckham at this stage, Nick."

"Ok. Thanks for the heads-up, Geth."

"What's new?" barked Randwick above the noise of the siren, his eyes wide, trying to weave through the sticky traffic.

"Gethin's got a DNA match from the bedroom and bathroom in the flat of our two vics from this morning."

"Good," said Randwick. "We are getting the right runaround today and it looks like it's about to get nasty down in New Cross."

Sands looked out of the window. He sensed a connection between all of these events. It was happening so fast there was little chance to join the dots. He also sensed danger as they sped towards the gun battle and he pictured his son, Sam, who would probably be enjoying some fish fingers.

"That woman from earlier, Dave," Sands started, blocking out the image of his son's tea-time.

Randwick threw the car violently to the left then cursed under his breath as they narrowly avoided a pedestrian who'd wandered into the traffic, seemingly mesmerised by his mobile.

SUNSET OVER SUNSET © Steve Richards

"Yeah. What about her?" Randwick called, swearing again as a white van threatened to pull out into his path.

"Where did she work again?" asked Sands.

"Sunset Club. Burlesque place up by Holborn."

"Previous?"

"Eh?" said Randwick, distracted. He briefly mounted the kerb to avoid an oncoming cyclist. "Er," he said trying to align his thoughts while weaving through the urban assault course.

"The Sunset," Randwick said, collecting his thoughts, "Yeah. Well, no. It's run by this Irish fella. Seamus something. I've been in once or twice. Smooth operator. Seems legit. Which virtually guarantees he's not."

Sands held the dashboard as the car swayed violently again.

"Call the Armed Response guys, Nick, can you?" asked Randwick, changing the subject. "See how they're doing. We don't want to walk into Helmand Province without the cavalry."

Back at the Italian cafe, Craig sat nursing his third cappuccino. Clive was outside on Craig's mobile again, updating Margaret as to why they would all be late home. He was then to call his old military cronies to finalise the plan. Craig watched Clive through the window. He was animated, obviously excited by the prospect of one more excursion behind enemy lines.

Craig looked at his watch. Anita had been gone a good half hour. He had tried to keep her out of proceedings but she had insisted on playing an active part. The one proviso to Clive was not to mention Anita's involvement to Margaret. Anita and Margaret had always got along famously and if his mum got an inkling of her involvement, she would cause havoc. She might have even called the police which, given their current plan, was now the last thing Craig wanted.

Anita suddenly bustled back into the cafe. She looked like she had had a mild electric shock. She was smiling and shaking her head. With a smile,

SUNSET OVER SUNSET © Steve Richards

she sat and held out her hand, "Philly Reid, nice to meet you."

Craig stared at her. Was he the only one not enjoying this?

"You didn't..." he started.

"I bloody well did," she said proudly. "I stormed it! There was this Eastern European guy who interviewed me. Ten minutes of chat and a quick walk up and down the stage, shaking my money-maker, and I start tonight!"

Craig was open-mouthed.

"I said that an old boyfriend had tipped me off," she added, "and I had popped in while I was passing. Pure coincidence. Lucky. I told him I had some experience working over in the States. Remember when we both went on holiday in New Orleans years ago?"

"Yeah," Craig said.

"Well, I imagined I was one of the performers in that burlesque show we went to. Remember?"

"Tell me you didn't do the accent..." Craig said, palming his forehead.

"No!" Anita retorted. "Philly's an all-Scottish minx," she said, slapping her thigh. Craig wondered if she was on Class A stimulants.

"Anyway, the American thing'll work because he won't be able to check up as they're seven hours behind. I only need work here one night after all." Anita reached over and playfully pressed the tip of Craig's nose with her index finger.

"Come on, big boy, we gotta roll with the punches," she said attempting an American accent which sounded like a mix of Australian and South African, with a mild Welsh undertone.

Craig stared at the woman who looked uncannily like his wife. She was amazing.

"I start at nine tonight," she beamed, "so I need to go back at 8pm-ish

SUNSET OVER SUNSET © Steve Richards

so the guy, Pieter I think, can give me the guided tour and show me my outfits."

It dawned on Craig for the first time that Anita was probably going to need to get topless in front of an audience. It was the equivalent of a Mother Superior turning up at a championship cage fighting event and demanding a tilt at the title.

"But..." Craig started, lowering his gaze to stare at her chest.

"It'll be fine!" she admonished. "Look, we need to get someone on the inside if we're going to work out what's going on, right? Right!?" she repeated to shake his gaze.

"Craig, there is merit in Clive's plan. Having been in, I'm sure there's something dodgy about the whole set-up over there and if I can help, now's the time to step up. I'd only worry anyway, so this way I can keep my eyes and ears open."

"It's not your eyes and ears I'm worried about," said Craig, returning his eyes southwards.

Clive bounded back into the Cafe. He looked at Anita anxiously. "All ok, dear?"

"Plain sailing, Major. I think I might be a natural." She shook her shoulders at him.

"My word, Craig. She's a keeper!" purred Clive. "Prepared to put her body on the line. Raaather!" he added, caressing his moustache.

"Right you two, nutters," Craig said, as Clive sat back down next to Anita.

"Let's go over this stupid plan one more time."

SUNSET OVER SUNSET © Steve Richards

29
Fools Russian In

Back in the comfort of his office, Seamus had visitors. His brother had arrived via the first flight into London City airport following his phone call that morning. He had met up with an old contact who had supplied a rare and plentiful range of guns, grenades and ammunition.

"Good trip?" Seamus asked over his shoulder, pouring five large measures of Bushmills whiskey into crystal tumblers. As he handed them round, his brother ignored the question.

"So what's this all about, wee man?"

Seamus hated being addressed by his childhood moniker, especially in front of others.

"I thought you boys could do with a nice little break in The Big Smoke," he said, "I remember it can get a little damp back home, weather-wise, so welcome to the bright lights in the big city, and that mythical thing you've seen on the telly called *sunshine*." His four visitors stared at him silently.

Seamus took a sip and put the tumbler down on his monolithic desk. HIs brother sat in the chair opposite, with his three men behind him. They were all in their forties and one might have turned fifty, but they made an impressive wall of flesh and bone. A wave of comfort and reassurance flooded through Seamus, reinforced by the warm glow from the whiskey. The men were all dressed in the requisite leather jackets, jeans and steel capped boots. Seamus noticed they had each been told to wear different colour t-shirts under their jackets to avoid looking immediately like the brutal group of professional thugs they were.

"I'm having one or two issues with the local competition," Seamus said, addressing his brother. "Over here, you've got the Yardies, the Eastern Europeans, the Cockneys and the Russians. Some of the Eastern Euros are bossed by the Russians. The old communist block lives on."

Seamus got up, plucking his drink from the desk. He walked around to the same side of the desk as his visitors in a conscious act of togetherness. He perched on the corner.

"The Yardies keep themselves to themselves. They sell largely to their own in the black areas of town. They pick off some of the clubs too but they steer clear of the centre."

Shaun and his men listened intently, sipping the whiskey intermittently.

Seamus continued with the briefing. "The Eastern Euros can get nasty but they tend to sell to the addicts. Bottom dollar for an inferior product. Again, they steer largely clear of the big central tourist areas which have been run by the cockney crews for the last couple of centuries."

Seamus swirled the viscous, neat spirit in his glass as he spoke.

"That's where I muscled in. They were careless. Lazy. Bloated by years of success. It was easier than I thought, to be honest. I bought this place then started small and gradually increased operations. They moaned and groaned a bit but I dealt with it.

"Donal, you remember Donal?" Seamus asked and was returned a nod. "Yeah, Donal moved to London and a few of his boys have been supporting me. Well trained. Disciplined. Good guys."

"What about the Russians?" asked Shaun, placing his empty tumbler on the desk.

"I was coming to that," Seamus said with a smile," Yes, the Russians concentrate on the high end market, supplying the casinos and the flash parts of town with coke and flesh. I've largely steered clear as they're ex-military men too. Choose your battles and all that. Well organised, unlike the others. There are a hundred and one other players but they're the major ones."

"So...?" Shaun prompted. The man really was no conversationalist.

"So...." Seamus repeated playfully, "The Yardies are good as gold so I leave them alone. The Eastern Euros too, for the large part. The Russians made a move for one of Donal's men but I saw it coming. I can't have that, can I?" Seamus smiled and took a sip. "Brisk and decisive."

He placed his empty glass on the desk as if squashing a bug.

"They were careless," he continued, "only sent one man for the move against my man so we took him. It happened to be the Russian Number Two. Some *Terminator* clone called Sergei. Took four of us to get him strapped to the chair."

Two of Shaun's men looked at each other disapprovingly. Seamus continued, noting their disdain. He needed to inspire confidence.

"Anyway, the fucker got lucky and we found out he was still alive. I intervened at the hospital to make sure the Russians thought it was the Cockneys."

He glanced at his watch. "Just about now, there should be a minor war going on down in south east London. So I took the precaution of inviting the local Bobbies to the party. If there's anyone left standing, the local police are going to ask a few questions. And if either crew manage to put two and two together," he lifted a finger to emphasise the next few words, "which I doubt, then there's a decent chance we might become rather popular."

He walked back round the other side of the desk and retook his seat. "You see, the Head Cockney's son - this little snarling runt of a cunt - popped by recently," Seamus reached forward to grasp the edge of the desk with his thumbs underneath.

"And..?" Shaun prompted again, impatiently. He was obviously surprised at the scale and seriousness of the situation he'd walked into.

"And...," Seamus said coolly, "I gave him the shock of his life," he feathered the switch under the desk and a very quick dart of electrical current invaded the chair opposite. Shaun leapt into the air with an involuntary yelp. The men behind him were immediately alert.

Seamus tried not to look smug but he couldn't help it. Shaun gave his brother a murderous stare.

SUNSET OVER SUNSET © Steve Richards

No one moved. Seamus started to think he might've misjudged his little prank. Shaun then turned around and took the tumbler from the man in the middle of the three stood behind him. He swallowed the remainder of the whiskey, maintaining his glare at Seamus from over the rim of the glass. As he swallowed, he lowered the glass and a wry grin formed along his lips.

"You little fecker."

"So get some rest, boys," Seamus said. "Nothing's going to happen tonight so rest up. It'll be tomorrow at the earliest that sparks start flying. I need you to add your particular skills to those of Donal's crew 'til the dust settles. I've reserved rooms for all of you round the corner at the Kingsway Hall Hotel. Nice and quiet. "

The men made to leave and Shaun asked Seamus, "Police?"

"Clueless, mainly," said Seamus. "There's one guy, though, who's not as stupid as the rank and file. 'Sands' is his name."

The Irishmen looked at each other.

 "I know," said Seamus, "as in 'Bobby'," he gave Shaun a raised eyebrow.

"Our Inspector Sands had an 'unfortunate accident' a few months ago. Stab-wound to the back," Shaun glanced back up at the hunting knives in the presentation case. "But I'm told he is thinking about a return to active service. We will need to keep an eye on him."

From behind the bar at The Sunset, Peter Pyptiuk watched the four burly men reappear into the main public area of the club. They had arrived half an hour earlier. Seamus told him to expect them so Pieter showed them straight in. Irish accents. Trouble afoot, Pieter thought. He sipped at a Red Bull over ice perched on a stool. He then rose to greet the new dancer to whom he had offered a job, more or less on a whim, a couple of hours earlier.

"Hi Philly," Pieter said warmly as she approached. He realised this

SUNSET OVER SUNSET © Steve Richards

probably wasn't her real name. The girls regularly took on a different persona the second they entered their work environment. Pieter noticed that she seemed slightly nervous, which also wasn't unusual. But this girl was slightly older than the usual performers so he would've expected a more confident persona. At the brief interview earlier, she had exuded confidence having performed in The States. Given the imminent arrival of the Irishmen, and with Seamus in furtive mood, Pieter had little appetite to vet his new recruit too vigorously. She seemed to know what she was doing.

He showed her into the dressing room and told her to choose an appropriate outfit from the range they kept in stock. "As I said earlier, you'll be doing hourly slots, on the hour. 8pm, then 10pm and midnight. Ten minutes each. Striptease, right?"

"Burlesque strip," Philly corrected, looking around the dressing room rather anxiously. Pieter wondered how different this set-up might be to what she was used to in the US.

"Everything ok?" he asked, reassuringly. "Er, yes, absolutely fine," she said. "Just trying to get my bearings."

"Listen, I've probably got enough cover tonight if you'd rather start tomorrow? It has been quite a quick turnaround..."

"No, no," Philly said quickly. "Tonight is absolutely fine."

"Ok," said Pieter, "I'll leave you to it. The other girls will start to arrive shortly, they'll show you the ropes."

"Just one thing," Philly asked. "You were going to give me a tour, were you not?"

Pieter looked at his watch and paused. He looked at Philly who stared back with big blue eyes. Pieter thought she was attractive. There was something unusual about her he couldn't yet work out.

"Ok," he relented. Follow me."

'Philly' followed Pieter who then indicated where to find the toilets, the

SUNSET OVER SUNSET © Steve Richards

stage entrances and exits, and the bar area. "That's the boss's office," he added, pointing to a door partially hidden down one of the private corridors. "Don't go in there unless specially invited. The boss-man doesn't like unexpected visitors."

Philly made an indelible mental note. The information was the only payment she was going to receive for her impromptu debut.

30
Special Delivery

The plan was relatively simple, on paper.

Clive and Craig had decamped from the Italian cafe to a local pub called the Prince of Wales on the corner of Great Queens St and Drury Lane. To anyone having a drink near London's fashionable Covent Garden, it would've looked like a father and son meeting up with a group of the father's old mates. The pub was relatively busy as it was a Thursday night.

Anita had already left to start her first shift at The Sunset. She had given Craig a warm and heart-felt hug before she left. Craig realised how much he really stood to lose if events in the next few hours went awry. No wife, no kids, no job, no prospects, not to mention the lack of liberty and abject misery at Her Majesty's Pleasure.

Clive's old contacts ('old' being the operative word) looked to Craig to be the walking embodiment of a euthanasia advert. Their average age must've been around 70. There were seven of them in total, including Clive. They all turned up promptly at the given time and all synchronised watches, out of habit rather than necessity as far as Craig could deduce. They exchanged a few pleasantries and handshakes but there was a general air of anxious anticipation. These men were obviously used to going on dangerous missions. The only problem in Craig's eyes was that it was no longer 1953.

Clive naturally took charge and called them to order. He repeated the plan that had obviously been cascaded via phone calls, and possibly ear trumpets, within the group. Clive used his fair share of military jargon and there was much nodding of heads and gnashing of dentures. Craig thought it might have been slightly endearing had it been the subject of a TV documentary instead of the forerunner to his almost inevitable lifelong incarceration.

To be fair, most of them looked to be in reasonable shape. At least there were no eye-patches or Zimmer frames and it wasn't obvious if any of them were packing a colostomy bag. One of them was actually wearing a beret but he just about carried if off. "Soft drinks all round," declared Clive, with the promise of brandies all round after the 'operation'.

Craig would've been more grateful if he had any genuine faith in their plan actually being successful. He had the feeling that he was a passenger on a steam train whose driver had no idea how to work the controls; a train that was about to be surrounded and derailed by some kind of helicopter gunship with superior technology, intelligence and firepower.

His mind wandered to Anita. He wondered about her current mental state, not to mention her current state of undress. She had put herself on the line for him. The least he could do was try to support Clive and his merry old band as much as he could.

At Clive's signal, they all stood and moved into the street. They followed one of the men - the shortest of the 'magnificent seven' - along Drury Lane and into a small mews where he had parked his car. It was a surprisingly quiet spot given they were in the heart of London's bustling West End. They formed a line behind the car - a 1977 maroon Mercedes in mint condition. The owner unlocked the boot, pulled it open and all eight of them leaned forward to peer inside.

Clive, again, took charge.

"Blooming Ada, Bremner," he said as they collectively perused the array of assault rifles, grenades and other hardware in front of them, "we're going to kidnap someone, not storm the Alamo," Clive gave the man a playful slap on the back.

"Be prepared," the man said in a Scottish accent, "any Cub Scout knows that." A giggle or two trickled around the line-up.

"Well these might be useful," Clive said leaning into the boot and lifting three coshes. "I think we should keep it rather 'light touch' on the firearms and projectile explosives front." He looked around the group and furnished the three largest men with the weapons. "Let's go with the coshes and see how we get on, eh. After all, it should be relatively plain sailing to get the boss man wrapped up and out of the club. He turned to face the tallest man among them, a man with a mane of

SUNSET OVER SUNSET © Steve Richards

perfectly coiffured silver-grey hair wearing an expensive-looking green wax jacket. "Ok, Flinty, time to mobilise the van. Bring it to sit outside the club."

"Bremner, you station yourself in the back of Flinty's van and be ready when we emerge with the target. Three knocks to open. Got it?"

"Sir!" acknowledged Flinty with a small salute. Craig thought he was joking. He wasn't.

Clive looked at his watch. "Ok, men. It's 19.52. We hit the club at twenty hundred hours. Any questions?" He handed round a ten pound note to each of the men who were going to enter the club.

"Here's your entry money. Just some old soaks on a pub crawl looking for some harmless titillation," he looked at Craig who made a face at Clive's turn of phrase.

"Oh, sorry, old boy. No offence." Craig held up a hand to indicate none had been taken. "You stick with Bremner and Flinty in the van, Craig. We don't want anyone in the club remembering us from earlier. I'll stay at the back of the group so they're unlikely to recognise me." He stroked his moustache with thumb and forefinger. "Ok, men. Let's go."

The archaic band of brothers walked purposefully along the road without a word. Craig hung back then noticed that the men in front of him almost immediately fell in to march in time with each other. Force of habit, he mused. He looked at his watch. He wondered how Anita was baring up.

Inside The Sunset Club, the first of Anita's three chosen tracks came on. Backstage, her legs were shaking. She was dressed in a black sequinned leotard, decorative black head-dress with three large black feathers protruding from the top. She was wearing black stockings and black high heels. In her hands, she held two huge feather fans which she planned to cover her modesty for the large part. She was the first act of the night to take to the stage and the audience was threadbare.

Only six men, a group of four and a group of two, were in attendance.

SUNSET OVER SUNSET © Steve Richards

Neither group seemed to pay much attention when Philly made her debut, kicking her legs to the music. She glanced over to the bar where Pieter, the man who had interviewed her earlier, was watching while drying a glass with a tea-towel.

After a few seconds, a wave of excitement and professional pride shuddered through her. She instinctively wanted to get the attention of the six men in the audience. She didn't like to be ignored. She also knew it was important to prove to Pieter that she was an experienced dancer or her cover would be blown. She knew she was on for ten minutes. She planned to bear all only in the final few seconds of her third song. She kicked then thrust her hips, shimmered her fan and no-one seemed interested.

She then noticed the arrival of five elderly gentlemen. Four sat at a table near the stage. Clive went to the bar to get some drinks as planned. She looked over to the bar. Pieter had disappeared. Clive was being served by a young girl she had never seen before. The first song segued into the second and she pointed the feather fans to the left, as planned, to indicate the direction of the boss's office which she had remembered from earlier. The elderly men seemed reassuringly attentive, captivated. One, she felt sure, was ogling her legs. At least she thought it was her legs. As she shimmied to the left, she caught a glimpse of Pieter making his way to the Boss's office. This wasn't in the plan.

She fretted as she shook her shoulders alluringly. The third track started and she noticed a smaller man emerge from the corridor of the office and move towards the exit. The elderly men didn't seem to notice. They were glued to Anita. One then glanced at his watch and nudged another by the elbow. Both immediately stood and moved towards the corridor. To Anita, it was like watching a car crash in slow motion. She could see exactly what was going to happen so she shook her head vigorously in time to the music, nodding like a chicken to the right. She then noticed the other men in the venue had started watching - obviously the unorthodox moves were causing a stir. To try to communicate her intentions to the elderly men, Anita stared at the two remaining old-stagers and moved to the right, shaking everything god gave her away from the corridor.

Out of the corner of her eye she saw Clive re-join the group and all three eschewed her signals and headed for the exit. Anita started to panic.

SUNSET OVER SUNSET © Steve Richards

Any allure she'd manage to muster during her performance ebbed away as she realised her third song was nearing its end and she hadn't revealed a thing.

She looked over at the bar. The small man who had earlier emerged from the corridor to the left of the stage was now emptying the dregs of a bottle of whiskey into a glass. He was staring at her. As the final bars of the song played out Anita dropped her feathers, pulled the front of her leotard down to her waist and as the final note sounded, thrust both arms into the air and threw her head back, staring skywards.

Behind the bar, Seamus had never seen anything like it. The final flourish and reveal from his new dancer made him miss the glass and pour the final drops of whiskey over his shoes. Anita saw him disappear behind the bar, as if looking for another bottle.

At the exact same moment, across the club, two elderly men were bundling a tall thin man out of the corridor and towards the exit. Their quarry was obscured by an old hessian sack which the men had placed over his head. In a few seconds the three had gone. Seamus stood back up to join his six remaining customers to see his new performer still frozen on the stage in mid-pose. The song had finished and the dancer looked like she was playing musical statues.

Seamus noticed she had a great body and very pale skin. He broke the silence by starting to clap. A couple of patrons started to join in half-heartedly and Anita was roused enough to reach hurriedly forward to grab the feather fans and scuttle off stage accompanied by a loud chicken impression trumpeted by one of the men at the back of the room.

Seamus made a mental note to ask Pieter where he'd found their new recruit.

Thirty metres away, an old soldier knocked out the man on reception at The Sunset Club with a cosh. He was facing the stairs and had not looked behind him when the man emerged silently from the club's main area.

SUNSET OVER SUNSET © Steve Richards

The trio waited for a minute and were then joined, as planned, by their two colleagues, trying to direct a man in a sack down the stairs. The six then stumbled into the street and towards the van parked right outside. A brisk three knocks on the back of the van and the doors swung open, one of them catching the person in the sack on the head with a sickening 'clonk'. They threw him inside and then clambered in to join him. Clive darted along the side of the van and slid into a seat in the front alongside the driver.

Before the back doors were properly shut, the van pulled violently out of the parking space. Craig had to grab the jacket of the man trying to close the doors to prevent him from being catapulted into the gutter.

"Bravo, boys!" Clive shouted over his shoulder to the men in the back, who were sat with their backs to the windowless sides of the van. At their feet, the man in the sack was groaning.

"All ok?" Craig enquired.

"Like clockwork," came the reply from one of the men.

"How was Anita?" Craig called forward to Clive.

"Beguiling," answered one of the men in the back with a wink.

"Clucking marvellous," added one of the others accompanied by a jerk of the head and a roar of laughter. Craig was struggling to see the funny side. Clive stepped in to save his blushes,

"Ok, boys, that's quite enough. In all seriousness, that was a good result. Just like old times."

Craig climbed forward to position his head just behind Clive's. In a hushed tone, laden with stress, he pleaded, "How did Anita do, really?"

"Well," he replied stroking his moustache, as if it would help to find the right word, "put it this way, Old Chap. She tried her best, gave it everything, but it wouldn't surprise me if this guy," he gently nodded backwards towards the prone figure at Craig's feet, "wasn't the only one getting sacked this evening." Another burst of laughter filled the van.

SUNSET OVER SUNSET © Steve Richards

Upstairs at The Sunset, Seamus waltzed straight into the changing room behind the stage. Two other girls were topless but didn't bat an eyelid. He approached his new recruit who was hammering a message into her mobile phone.

"Unusual act," Seamus said from directly behind Anita who almost jumped out of her skin. She hurriedly obscured the message.

"Uh, oh, hi!" Anita exclaimed. "Er, thank-you," she added as Seamus helped her remove her flamboyant head-dress, their hands touching briefly.

"Where are my manners?" said Seamus, smiling smoothly, holding out a hand.

"I'm Seamus Twite, the owner." Anita swallowed hard and took his hand firmly and shook it. She was not totally unused to being blindsided by smug, powerful males. Her office in Edinburgh was full of them.

"Ani…" she started before correcting herself, "…Philly Reid. Nice to meet you." Anita felt the man's stare cut through her pretence, peeling away layers of deceit with every lingering second. "Where did you learn the, er," he nodded back towards the stage, "'act?'"

Anita stood up to try to level the imbalance of power. She mustered a semblance of conviction in her reply, "In the States, actually. The Deep South."

"Hmm," Seamus mused, "they love their chicken down there, I guess?" Anita's cheeks flushed.

"Well, it's my first night, Seamus. So I'll need to acclimatise to a UK audience."

He moved towards her and she thought for a horrifying moment he was going to kiss her. Instead, he gently took a stray feather from her hair.

"Thank you," she repeated. Anita knew instinctively this man was full of menace. But at the same time his tone and movements hinted at a softer

SUNSET OVER SUNSET © Steve Richards

side. She also noticed the two girls who had shared the dressing room had now disappeared and she was alone with the man she suspected of double murder.

Silence reigned. Anita felt Seamus stare straight into her soul.

Back in the main Club, loud music suddenly started up. The next act must be on. It broke the awkwardness just enough for Anita to say, "I really should be getting a little something to eat before I'm back on. She started to put a jacket over her t-shirt and tucked her phone into her jeans pocket. "I haven't eaten for hours." Again, Seamus moved towards her. This time he took the far shoulder of her jacket and he obligingly helped her put her other arm in.

"Thanks," she said.

"My pleasure," he said. She moved quickly towards the exit, conscious not to appear to be bolting.

"Come back soon," he called after her. "I, for one, can't wait for the second instalment." Just as she reached the door, he added, "Oh, Ani," a chill ran through her as he used the shortened version of her real name.

"You haven't seen Pieter by any chance have you? He seems to have disappeared."

"Haven't seen him," she called over her shoulder pushing at the door to leave. Seamus stroked the feathery head-dress.

"Curiouser and curiouser," he said under a raised eye-brow.

SUNSET OVER SUNSET © Steve Richards

31
Duty Calls

Sands and Randwick jogged up the stairs of The Sunset Club to find a man on the front desk with a bag of ice on the back of his neck. He was being nursed by a young girl who was gently stroking the top of his shoulders.

"All ok?" asked Randwick sarcastically. The man and woman both shot him a look that would curdle milk.

"Migraine?" asked Sands.

"Or something a little more sinister?" continued Randwiick, displaying his police ID.

"Go get Seamus," the man with the headache said to the woman, who immediately shuffled away after giving the two policemen the best glare she could summon.

"Don't worry," said Randwick, in pursuit of the girl, "we'll introduce ourselves to him in person."

As they entered the main area of the club, Seamus was already waiting to greet them. An act was performing on stage, this time two girls engaged in a bizarre contortionist double-act without a bra between them.

"Good evening, gentlemen," Seamus said congenially. "Shall we?" he held out an arm to usher them down the corridor towards his office.

"First on the left" he said, following the two men. "It's not true what they say, is it?" Seamus said.

"What's that?" replied Randwick.

"There's never a policeman around when you need one," Seamus said, "Then they're everywhere when you don't."

The two investigators entered the office then paused for Seamus to come from behind them and direct the room. "Please take a seat, gentlemen," said Seamus, again waving them towards his intended direction. They sat opposite his chair.

"Drink?" said Seamus.

"N...." began Sands.

"Ah no," interrupted Seamus, "the police are tee-total these days. I should've remembered." Sands bristled at the air of confidence exuded by the man they'd come to question.

Seamus collected a glass tumbler containing whiskey that was sat on the far side of the desk, sitting in his chair opposite the policemen.

Randwick began, "Mr Twite...."

"Such formality! Call me 'Seamus', please, Detective Sergeant Randwick."

Randwick was momentarily thrown by the fact the Irishman opposite him remembered his name. It had been more than a year since he had last visited.

Randwick continued, "There have been a series of events that have unfolded in the last 24 hours or so that are most troubling."

"Tell me about it," said Seamus sardonically.

"Well we were rather hoping you might do just that," Sands piped up.

"Ah, Inspector Sands, I was wondering when we might hear from you," said Seamus over a sip of whiskey. "Good to see you back at work. Terrible burden on the taxpayer, you know. All of these public servants spending months 'off sick,'" he embellished the final two words with flicks of his forefingers to write quote marks in the air.

Randwick gave his partner a sideways glance. His teeth were gritted and the muscle in his jaw was twitching wildly. He jumped into the conversation to try to get back on track.

"Look, Mr Twite," Seamus shook his head slightly but Randwick ignored him and continued, "as I'm sure you're aware - and you do seem to be terribly well informed - there has been a major falling out down in New Cross between two rival gangs. I don't suppose..."

Seamus leaned forward to deposit his glass on his desk with a jolt.

"All very interesting I'm sure," said Seamus dismissively, "but the reason I'm glad you're here, officers, is that I believe I've been the victim of a kidnapping."

"Mr Twite!" shouted Randwick starting to lose his temper. Seamus held up his index finger to silence him.

"You're not listening, Detective Sergeant. One of my staff was, not 15 minutes ago, bundled into a sack and taken away by what looked on my CCTV to be several members of *Dad's Army*. Now I'd like report this as a crime and demand you make it a top priority."

Sands snarled, "You are in no position to demand anything of us, Sir."

Seamus rocked back in his chair, staring back at Sands. After a short pause, he leaned forward and put both hands on the desk, palms down, thumbs under the lip of the desk.

"Do you feel it?" he asked Sands.

"What?"

"I feel a certain degree of electricity between you and I, Inspector Sands?"

Randwick had had enough. It was time to throw in the verbal hand grenade.

"Mr Twite, do you happen to know the whereabouts of another of your employees? She is Claire Jones, known to you, we believe, as Destiny." Randwick and Sands both scoured Twite's face to gauge his reaction. He stared back at them implacably. Not a flicker. Randwick thought this man would be a decent poker player. Seamus paused to choose his reply carefully.

"I have no idea where Destiny is. I was going to ask Pieter if she'd booked the day off but this is going to be reasonably tricky as he has been bundled off the premises by armed assailants. And the police don't seem remotely interested."

"Mr Twite," deadpanned Randwick, "Destiny was found dead this morning. We have reason to believe she was murdered."

This time, Seamus reacted. He frowned and picked up his whiskey as if to comfort him against the news. Sands thought he looked genuinely shocked and troubled by the news.

"So do you happen to know if Destiny was in any kind of trouble?" Sands asked. "Do you know why anyone might have wanted to harm her?"

"She's a sweet, she *was* a sweet girl." He drained the last of his whiskey, frowning hard. Randwick made a mental note to add method acting to Seamus's burgeoning list of talents.

Sands pressed on, "Can you please answer the question, Mr Twite."

"Which one?" he shot back. "You asked me two fucking questions." The first flash of aggression from Twite. He lurched forward and slammed his glass back on the desk. Randwick and Sands both jumped. Staring directly at Sands, Seamus hissed, "No. The answer to both your questions is 'no.'"

He stood up. "So unless you're arresting me, I'd like to be alone with my thoughts." He started to walk around the desk towards the two seated policemen who looked at each other. Randwick took the lead.

"Mr Twite, we would like to take you to the station to answer some more questions, if that's ok."

"That is most definitely not ok, DS Randwick. Not at all. Unless you hadn't noticed, it would appear I am now two staff members down so I need to be here to run my business."

SUNSET OVER SUNSET © Steve Richards

"But, Mr Twite," started Randwick but then stopped as Seamus moved to stand directly in front of him menacingly. Sands felt a bolt of adrenalin rush through him. His phone vibrated. He glanced at the text.

"DS Randwick, I have asked you already. Are....you...arresting...me?" Twite's face was now bright purple. He jutted out his jaw, adding, "I would have thought it a fairly clear and reasonable question in the circumstances."

Randwick stared into Seamus's eyes. "Don't go anywhere. We will be watching you, Mr Twite. Expect to see us again very soon." The two officers made for the door.

Just as they were about to leave, Sands stopped and turned around to face the club boss.

"One final thing, Mr Twite. I notice one of the hunting knives in your collection is missing," Sands pointed to the presentation case on the wall. Randwick noticed it for the first time. Seamus walked towards Sands who braced himself.

With his face no more than three inches from Sands, Seamus said "I noticed that too, Inspector. Perhaps you might be able to add theft to kidnapping and murder on your list of pressing priorities."

He then reached up, put his hand on Sands' shoulder and exerted enough pressure to turn the policeman's body around towards the door to usher him out. "A hunting knife in the wrong hands can be a very dangerous weapon, you should know that better than most," Seamus added, tapping Sands on the back in the exact place where he had been stabbed months earlier.

A shiver went down Sands' spine and the colour drained from his face. As they exited the main floor and reached the top of the stairs, Randwick said, "We are going to nail that bastard, Nick."

"I sincerely hope so," replied Sands, maintaining his composure, "but first we need to get back to St Thomas's. That text said that the Russian is talking."

Across town in Islington, the old soldiers had extricated their prisoner, still in the sack, from the van and sat him on a chair in an empty double garage of a townhouse just north of Upper Street near Angel tube station. They surrounded him in a circle. Craig looked at the obscured body and thought something didn't look right. Clive reached forward and pulled off the sack.

Pieter blinked back at him, his eyes adjusting to the light. Clive turned around to face Craig who met his gaze by uttering "Fuck...in...hell."

"Shitting tits," said Clive looking back to peruse their quarry.

"What?" enquired Bremner.

"It's the wrong sodding bloke!" shouted Craig, his frustration boiling over.

"He was in the office, where you said," moaned the tallest man, Flinty.

"He might well have been, but he's not our man," said Clive, wiping the back of his hand across his moustache.

Craig's mobile rang. It was Anita. He stepped away from the group to speak more privately.

"Craig," she said, her voice cracking with emotion.

'What?" Craig asked, rubbing his brow furiously.

"I'm ok. I'm ok." she said. Craig pictured her. This was not her problem. It was all his fault. Anita should be in Edinburgh wrestling with the corporate elite rather than risking everything with some bloody gangsters in London to save her husband's neck. She continued, "I think the old guard might've kidnapped the wrong guy." She sounded close to tears.

"Where are you?" asked Craig. His stress level peaked.

"It's ok, Craig," she said reassuringly, trying to offset her husband's worry. "I'm outside the club now. I got away. But not without an intense conversation with the owner-guy, Seamus,"

SUNSET OVER SUNSET © Steve Richards

"Did he touch you...? 'Cos if he...." Craig blurted.

"Calm down, Craig," she retorted. "I told you. I'm fine. He is an evil bastard, though, Craig. Pure evil. He spoke to me like he knew everything about me. It creeped me out."

"Well done for getting away. Just come here. I'll give you the address," he said. "And you're right. *Dad's Army* lifted the wrong fucking bloke. We have the barman guy here. Another sprinkle of fuck-up on the cake of shite I've been baking. I am so sorry, Ani."

"Craig," she interrupted, "Listen to me. You need to decide if you still need me as an insider in the club. I'm happy, well, not 'happy' perhaps, but prepared to go back there if you need me to. I've got more performances scheduled tonight. We need to finish what we've started."

Craig marvelled at the bravery and resourcefulness of his Missus. He felt an intense desire to hold her in his arms. "Ok. Can I call you back in five?"

"Ok," she said.

"Anita," Craig started, but she'd disconnected. He put the phone back into his pocket and turned back towards the barman and his captors.

Clive came over to Craig. "How's the old girl bearing up," he said as sympathetically as he could.

"She's ok," Craig said. "She needs to know whether we still need her inside the club. What's this bloke saying?"

"Well it's quite strange, actually," said Clive. "He's, well, being, what you might describe as unexpectedly co-operative'."

Clive leaned in closer to avoid being heard by the others who seemed to have exhausted their conversation with Pieter.

"He seems to appreciate we weren't after him and that it was an honest mistake. He's actually said he wants to help us if Seamus really is behind the death of his colleague, this Destiny girl. I think he might've liked her."

SUNSET OVER SUNSET © Steve Richards

"You told him about Destiny?!"

"Well we had to give him some sort of explanation! You were on the bloody phone!" Clive paused, lowering his tone. He sensed his old comrades were getting restless. "Why don't you talk to him?"

Craig looked over at the guy sat on the chair. He seemed cool as a cucumber. He was tall, skinny and pasty-white. Craig scratched the back of his head as if it would diffuse some of the pressure he was feeling. He walked over to the group.

"Ok," he started. "I understand the predicament has been explained to you. Destiny has been murdered. I was one of the last to see her alive. I think your boss is a nasty bastard who might have killed her. The girl called Philly who you interviewed earlier today is my wife. Her real name is Anita. She took the job to try to get us an insider's view. Seamus has just had a little private chat to her and she's bricking it. Clive says you're being awfully good about all of this. If I was you, I'd be pretty upset if I was put in a sack and bundled into a van."

"Look," Pieter said, "if what you say is true, and Destiny really is dead, and Seamus is guilty, I want to take the bastard down as much as you do. Destiny was a good friend of mine. I had no idea she had been killed until your man here," he pointed towards Clive, "just told me." He looked shocked and saddened. "The man you were really trying to lift," Pieter continued, "Seamus, has been acting strangely in recent days. He has just met with some reinforcements from his homeland back in Ireland. Something is brewing. Some trouble. Big stuff, I think. If he has hurt Destiny, I will help you." He looked intensely pained by the loss of his friend.

Clive looked at Craig. He was tempted to step in but Craig looked to have the bit between his teeth.

"Right," said Craig to the whole group, warming to his task. "We are not going to take down this man on our own. We need help, especially if he has his own cavalry on the doorstep. We also need to get some evidence that Seamus is guilty. That is going to be tricky."

Pieter piped up again, "It might be difficult but there is something that

SUNSET OVER SUNSET © Steve Richards

might help." The eight men stared at him intently. "I noticed earlier that one of Seamus's hunting knives had gone missing from his presentation case in his office." Craig's heart jumped. "If we can find the knife and link it to the murders, and to Seamus, we might have him. But god only knows where the knife is now..."

"I might have a clue on that front," said Craig. "We might actually be getting somewhere at last."

Craig's phone rang. It was Anita. "And...?" she said impatiently. Craig looked at Clive who nodded slowly.

"I think it would be useful if you go back in, Ani, but it's entirely up to you. No one is going to ask you to risk anything. If you want to steer clear, just go straight to my mum's flat. In fact, if you can find somewhere to wait, a pub of something around there, we'll come and pick you..."

"Ok, I'm going back in," came Anita's flat, unemotional reply.

"Wait. Looks like we're going to have this Pieter guy - the bar manager - to help us," said Craig. "He thinks Seamus might've murdered the girl too...."

"But if I just leave, he'll start to suspect something."

"Someone just kidnapped one of his staff, Ani. I think he might just start to have an inkling all's not rosy in the garden."

"Fair point. But if it can help to give us an edge, I'll go back. I don't mind. Really..."

Craig looked at Clive again, seeking help. Clive nodded again. Craig closed his eyes. "Ok, Ani, go back in. We'll be waiting around the corner to the right of the club when you come out. What time?"

"Should be all set by 12.15. See you then."

"Ok. Thanks, Ani. Love you loads..." But she'd already gone.

SUNSET OVER SUNSET © Steve Richards

32
Dot to Dot

The light was fading as Randwick and Sands raced back across town. As Randwick drove, Sands started to piece together the puzzle in his head.

Twite's reaction to news of Destiny's murder was inconclusive but Sands had the feeling there was something else going on. The sinister pat on the back also confirmed to him that Twite had been behind his own personal brush with mortality several months before. He tried to pinpoint why Twite's men had come after him. Sure, Randwick and Sands had dropped in on him once before over a year ago, but they were merely door-stepping him to see what they could find out.

The Jamaicans had started to moan about a new player sweeping up and while Randwick and Sands thought it could be Twite, no one was willing to give them anything to go on. They had set the trap at the jewellery store and taken all the usual precautions around setting it up. No one outside of the small circle within CID knew about it. Somehow Twite had been tipped off and he had lashed out at Sands and his colleague to murderous affect.

Sands was sure that Twite would not have personally been anywhere near the smash and grab. And he was pretty sure none of his henchmen would've talked to implicate Twite if they'd been caught. He was also certain it had not been Twite himself who had stabbed him then driven off on the motorbike. But Twite was pulling the strings; the master puppeteer who had moved to take out the man with the audacity to try to outsmart him in an ambush. The main gangs would tend to avoid rattling the police's cage but Twite had obviously not been able to deal with the affront. And he covered his tracks well - Sands knew that the investigation into his stabbing had turned up very little.

Randwick and Sands flashed their IDs at two new officers guarding the hospital room containing the large Russian with the badly bruised eye, thick ear and puncture wound in his neck. The man they perused in front of them propped up in the hospital bed, connected to two drips, was a large muscular hard-man in his early 40s. He looked to be asleep. A nurse arrived to change one of the drips as Randwick and Sands circled the bed.

"Is he sedated?" Randwick asked as the nurse efficiently went about her business.

"Yes," she said in a quiet, almost reverential voice, "heavily." She looked at Randwick. "This man is very ill. He lost a huge amount of blood and almost died. He will be very weak for the next 48 hours. You might be better off at least giving it until the morning."

"Thank you, nurse," said Randwick, pre-occupied. Sands' eyes flitted around the room.

"What do you reckon?" Randwick asked his partner. Sands thought for a moment, passing a cursory glance over the information on the charts at the bottom of the Russian's bed. "I'm not sure we're going to get any show tunes from our man here anytime soon."

The man stirred. Grimacing as he shifted his weight. Randwick took it as his cue.

"Sergei," he said, stooping to lower his head nearer to the prone man. "Sergei," he repeated, slightly louder. "Can you hear me?" Sands examined the drips disinterestedly. The man let out a groan and opened his good eye. "Sergei," Randwick said, more urgently. "Stay with me, soldier. Who did this to you?"

The man contorted his face in pain. Randwick leaned further down, his face two inches from the stricken Russian. "Who did this to you, Sergei?"

"Fgmrrrgh," moaned the man. "Frrrggmmrggh." Sands looked at his watch. A more senior nurse entered the room. She was bustling with officiousness.

"Gentlemen!" she barked. "This man is very unwell." She physically pushed Randwick backwards as she checked the man's hands to see if the drip feeds were stable. She continued, "You've had more time than is wise so I think you should come back tomorrow if you really need to.

This man needs his rest."

Sands pushed open the door wearily. They walked back towards the waiting room. "Earlier," he said to Randwick, "when we were here before...." He looked at Randwick who appeared lost in thought, wiping the tiredness from his face with a mop of his brow. "I reckon I saw Seamus Twite leaving this hospital when we arrived."

Randwick looked back at him. "What?"

"Thinking back," Sands repeated, "I'm sure I saw that bastard Twite exiting as we arrived. I didn't recognise him at first as it had been over a year since I'd seen him. Seeing him earlier has jogged my memory. I'm sure it was him."

"And...?" prompted Randwick as they entered the car park.

"Well, why would he be here?" said Sands impatiently. "Could he have found out that Sergei was still alive and be paying him a quick visit to finish what he'd started?" He now had Randwick's full attention. They got into the car and sat without starting the engine. "Could Twite have tipped off the guy that runs the Russians...what's his name?"

"Dmitri Usanov," said Randwick.

"Could he have been here to finish off Sergei," then got word to Dmitri that it was Blanchard's crew who were to blame. That would've triggered the war earlier in New Cross." Randwick stared straight ahead, thinking. Sands continued, "Twite then tips off Donny to expect trouble, guaranteeing a fair fight, with maximum casualties."

"Two birds, one stone." said Randwick.

"Exactly." said Sands. He shifted in his seat to face towards Randwick. "Seamus Twite doing what he loves doing: Pulling strings."

"But do you think he killed his bird, this...Destiny girl and her pal?" asked Randwick.

"He's certainly nasty enough. It looked like his personal handiwork too.

SUNSET OVER SUNSET © Steve Richards

I got a call earlier from a contact I'd asked for information in Northern Ireland and, guess what, a 'Seamus Twite' was a fully qualified surgeon for a brief period in the 90s. He left suddenly to go 'overseas'. Apparently he told his colleagues he was off to the States to perform plastic surgery on rich widows."

"Looks like he might've stayed to do some nips and tucks nearer home," said Randwick.

"I'm not sure about the missing hunting knife in the cabinet, though. It's too sloppy. Not like him."

"We don't even know if that's the murder weapon, do we?" mused Randwick. "Let's regroup in the morning," he added. "S'been one hell of a day."

Sands had a sudden yearning to hear the voice of his son but it was late and Sam would be tucked up in bed, a million miles from all the violence, murder and skulduggery that his dad had encountered on his first day back at work. As Randwick dropped him back at his flat, Sands thought back to his own stabbing. How had he known about the set-up? Seamus was very well informed. If he knew all about Sands and his whereabouts, he might also know about his son.

Sands suddenly wished that Sam really was a million miles away from all this and not just down the road in south London.

33
Pulling the Lion's Tail

Craig awoke next morning on a camp bed in the lounge of his mother's flat. He had slept like a log, tiredness enveloping him the second his head hit the pillow adorned with floral pillowcase. For a second, he felt refreshed. Then he looked to his right and saw his wife asleep on the sofa and the horrors of the previous 24 hours came flooding back.

He knew his saving grace had been the lack of a criminal record. If his DNA found at the murder scene had been fast-tracked and it had been matched to a profile on the criminal database, they could have traced him quite easily to his mother's flat. The fact that they hadn't been raided overnight lead Craig to be thankful for his law-abiding nature.

He also knew that there was an excellent chance this would be the day he would be incarcerated, charged and taken to prison where he would remain for the rest of his life. 'Sobering' didn't really do the thought justice. 'Fucking terrifying' was closer but still not quite representative.

He looked over again at Anita. She looked peaceful, her porcelain-pale smooth skin almost translucent in the light peeking through the curtains. The door to the lounge creaked slightly as it opened and his mother made a sign for him to join her in the kitchen.

Clive had not stayed over, but Craig quickly realised that he had become a regular guest in recent months. Last night, they'd dropped off Pieter and Clive's cronies in central London and picked up Anita from the club. On the drive back to Margaret McGill's flat, Clive, Craig and Anita had devised the plan for today.

Craig padded quietly through to the kitchen, keen to not disturb his wife.

"Morning, love," Margaret said as Craig entered the small kitchen. She handed him a cup of tea and they sat at a small table just inside the door. Craig sipped and winced at the heat of the steaming liquid on his lips and tongue.

Margaret was wearing a pink-checked housecoat with Craig in crumbled Rolling Stones t-shirt and boxer shorts.

"Wonder what the old man would've made of all this?" Margaret said softly. Craig blinked back at her, numbed by the question.

"Dunno," he managed as he pictured his old man. He could feel emotion rise in his throat and the knot tighten in his stomach. "It'll be alright," soothed Margaret. "Things'll sort themselves out. They always do." But Craig was in a reflective rather than receptive mood.

"But what if they don't, Mum?"

He lowered his voice, glancing back at the direction of the lounge containing his slumbering wife. "This has been a total car crash from the second I discovered the bodies yesterday morning." Margaret reached forward to stroke his arm sympathetically.

Craig continued, "Clive means well, mum, but you should've seen him yesterday. It was like he was taking part in some war game with his jolly old chums. I mean, who the hell IS this guy anyway?"

Margaret withdrew her arm from Craig. She stared at the floor then looked directly into Craig's eyes with fierce determination. "Look, Craig, it's about time you heard a few home truths here." She leaned forward. "In the past two years you've barely been near me. I know you're busy but I've been an old lady in a big old town and I've been lonely. In recent months, Clive has come into my life and enriched it enormously. Yes, he has his….ways…but he's decent, Craig. A decent man who didn't think twice about trying to help you yesterday in your hour of need. You were desperate. You still are. And let's face it, you're not entirely the innocent victim in all of this."

Craig recoiled. But Margaret continued, "Yes, you can act all hurt but as far as I can see it, you disappeared back to some girl's flat late at night. You say you hardly knew her but put yourself in Anita's shoes. How easy must that have been to believe?"

Craig opened his mouth, "B..."

SUNSET OVER SUNSET © Steve Richards

"Let me finish!" Margaret shot back, instantly lowering her raised voice with an anxious glance towards the lounge. "I know things between you two have been strained. Women worry about this type of thing. I used to worry when your father went away for those business trips. Yes, I trusted him but you still worry. You can't help it."

Craig had been silenced. He crossed his arms. Margaret softened her tone.

"You need to see things from other people's perspectives, son." She leaned forward to touch his elbow. "People care about you. We all do. That's why we're all trying to help. So all I'm saying is embrace their help. Help us to help you. Don't start firing off rounds at Clive. Or Anita. Or me." Craig stared at the steam coming from his tea.

"Unless we help to pull you out of this, you're staring into a big black hole and we will lose you..." Her voice cracked with emotion, "...and I couldn't face that, Craig." She lowered her head. "I just couldn't."

Anita entered the kitchen, having been eavesdropping.

"Me neither, Craig," she added. "We all need to work together to get through this." She paused. "Or we're FUCKED!"

Her emphasis on the final word caused them all to laugh out loud, Margaret, shrieking at the first expletive she had ever heard leave the mouth of her daughter-in-law.

Craig stood and gave his mother and wife a collective hug then picked up his tea.

"Ok, Thelma and Louise, lecture received and understood. You're right. Both of you." Craig looked at his mum. "I have neglected you since you moved down. It can't have been easy. And I reacted immaturely when I found out about Clive although some of that was, admittedly, due to the sight I saw protruding in his trousers."

He turned to Anita. "And I have been a selfish prick too with respect to you. There's you dropping everything to fly south to try to help, not even mentioning the fact I went back to a female stranger's flat at midnight and readily getting your Bristol Cities out at a moment's notice in a club

SUNSET OVER SUNSET © Steve Richards

run by a certifiable nutcase."

He took a step back so he could address both of them.

"If I had either of your courage or common sense, I'd have probably called the police first thing yesterday and things might've looked a lot rosier right now. So I'm sorry. Today I'm going to pull my head out of my arse and try to make a better fist of being a loving son and dutiful husband."

"So let's get at it, shall we," he added, taking a last sip of his tea and rubbing his hands together with a smile. "Time for a shower and a trip to the crematorium for me while you, Mum, find a swear box for my potty-mouthed wife here." He pecked Anita on the cheek and hopped off towards the bathroom.

Back in central London, Seamus had decided to meet with his brother and his full crew of eight professional hard men over breakfast at the club, including Donal's local team of four. They had some issues to discuss and they drank strong coffee with bacon rolls in the main area rather than in Seamus's office. The club was otherwise empty with a few empty glasses strewn across deserted tables.

"First things first," said Seamus, leaning forward in his chair and taking control. "The Russian in the hospital is dead. Died in his sleep overnight. Tragic shame. Loose end tied up. Apparently one of the nurses attached the wrong drip. Coma. Death. Drip detatched and incinerated."

"Best thing you ever did, getting that wee black nurse on the payroll," said Shaun. "Is she reliable?"

Seamus immediately knew his brother was asking if he wanted him to kill the nurse to silence her. He thought for a second, as if wondering which starter to pick on a menu, and shook his head. "Na," he said. "She was tricky to find and we might need her again in coming weeks and months. To be fair to her, she hasn't put a foot wrong up to now."

"So what's next?" asked Shaun, slurping at his hot coffee.

SUNSET OVER SUNSET © Steve Richards

"Item 2: Pieter, my bar manager," said Seamus. Shaun squinted. "You know, the tall dopey-looking European cunt behind the bar." Shaun nodded in recognition. "He was bundled out of here in a sack last evening by a group of pensioners soon after you lot left."

Shaun lurched forward, speaking through a mouthful of bacon, "You fucking what?! Kidnapped? From here?" he looked around the club. "By pensioners?! Where the fuck were you?"

"I was behind the bar at the time. They took him from my office. Pieter was in there fixing a lamp. They must've been after me. I only noticed afterwards when I rewound the CCTV and then found my door-man rubbing the back of this thick head. He'd been coshed by the group of old guys."

Shaun smirked, raised his eyebrows and shook his head "Someone's taking the piss out of you, Seamus, so they are." He rocked back in his chair staring at his brother. The others looked on as the brothers clashed horns. "In a sack!?" Shaun added. "Fuckin hell, Wee Man. Keystone fucking Cops!"

The back of Seamus's neck started to prickle. Shaun was the only man in the world who could talk to him like that and get away with it but not in front of others, Seamus couldn't have that.

"Well you'll get your chance to show us all how it's done, Shaun, and soon enough." Shaun's men stared with contempt at Donal and his guys. Seamus began to regret his decision to call for reinforcements.

"It's time to go to work," said Seamus.

Down in south east London, Donny Blanchard was calling a number he'd had to try very hard to get. "Dmitri?" Donny said when the call connected. "Is that you, Dmitri?"

"Who is this?" snarled the voice at the other end of the phone, in clipped Russian accent.

"It's the man you were trying your best to kill yesterday afternoon down in New Cross."

SUNSET OVER SUNSET © Steve Richards

Silence.

"Blanchard?" Dmitri asked. "How the fuck you have the nerve to call me? My god, I will make it my personal mission to cut off your head, you filthy fucking...."

"Dmitri," interrupted Donny. "Someone is playing us for mugs."

Silence again. "What do you mean?"

"Well, it would seem to me that you and your boys were pretty unhappy about something yesterday. It's a good job the armed police turned up when they did or we'd have all facking killed each other. Since then, I've found out about Sergei being in the hospital." More silence. "So I'm guessing something – or someone - led you to believe we'd put him there. So I'm calling to tell you, 100%, that it..."

"Sergei is dead," spat Dmitri.

"Oh, facking hell," said Donny, wiping his brow with a huge left hand. "What I'm trying to tell you, Dmitri, is that it wasn't our crew. God's honest. Someone set us up to take each other out. And I've got a good idea who that might be."

"Why should I believe you, you shit. I got the information on good authority," said Dmitri. "I was at the hospital myself. One of the doctors told me himself."

It was Donny's turn to pause. "Well I dunno where he got that idea, spare I don't."

"Who is to blame?" asked Dmitri. There was a delay at the other end as Dmitri pushed the phone more tightly towards his ear. Still no reply.

Down in Beckenham, Shaun picked up Donny's phone from the carpet. It was still connected. He pressed the red button to end the call and made the signal for his men to follow him towards the exit. Donny's lifeless body had slumped forward in his armchair. The bullet had entered his temple and he had died instantly. Shaun walked towards the wall where the bullet had embedded itself after passing through Donny's skull. He

SUNSET OVER SUNSET © Steve Richards

used a silver steel spike to remove the slug and he put it in his jacket pocket. He then unscrewed the silencer of his revolver and followed the men out of the French doors and onto the patio of Donny's large house.

SUNSET OVER SUNSET © Steve Richards

34
Showtime

Nick Sands got up early and drove across London to his son's adopted family home to see him before he went to school. Anil had opened the door with a huge smile and a cup of coffee to welcome his brother-in-law.

Sam and his dad spent a blissful 20 minutes asking questions about everyday mundane things that concern the average eight year-old (times tables, football stickers and crisps). Sands had known it could only be a brief catch-up but since his return to work the day before, he had recovered the confidence to meet his son face-to-face.

"Pickled onion Monster Munch? Oldy but a goody, I'll give you that," Sands said to his son in mock seriousness, shaking his head gently, "but to my mind, there is only one Wotsits."

Sam embraced his dad, putting his head on his shoulder. Anil peeked in, reluctant to break up the happy moment. Sands raised his eyebrows towards Anil who nodded.

"Ok, Sam," said Sands, pulling his son away from him, hands on shoulders to make eye contact, "time for school, little man. Time to run rings around your teachers."

"Thanks for coming, Dad," said Sam softly. "I'm glad you went back to work. The bad guys will be scared now."

"Well, I'm not sure about that," said Sands as his son wandered towards his uncle. "Shall I come across again on Sunday?"

"You'd bloody better," interjected Anil, ruffling Sam's hair, "those cricket tickets don't pay for themselves."

As his phone rang, Sands gave Anil a silent thumbs-up as his brother-in-law withdrew to take Sam to school with his cousins.

It was Randwick with some bad news.

"Sergei the Russian's dead, didn't make it through the night."

Randwick heard a muffled reply of 'Jesus' and he pictured Sands scratching his eyebrows, as he tended to do in response to stressful news.

"But the hospital said he'd pull thr..." protested Sands.

"I know," interrupted Randwick. "Something's not right there but it'll have to wait. I've also just had a phone message from the office saying they've had a call from an anonymous guy who says he was the man in the flat whose DNA we found at the scene yesterday morning; Destiny and the black guy."

"Crank?" asked Sands automatically.

"Well, I thought so too but the message also mentioned Seamus Twite so I think we'll call him back when we're together. See you at the station?"

"Give me half an hour," agreed Sands.

Across town, a large black Range Rover equipped with a reinforced bull-bar pulled out of a parking space and accelerated down a side street. The man in the passenger seat studied his iPad showing a map with a dot in the centre moving slowly along.

"Left, then second right," said the passenger to the driver who complied. The car stopped at a junction then pulled onto a main road with traffic lights up ahead. "Black Audi diagonally opposite," said the passenger. "There!" he said urgently and the Range Rover pulled out of the column of traffic onto the wrong side of the road then accelerated powerfully across the intersection towards the Audi.

At the last second, the driver of the Audi tried to turn away from the oncoming vehicle but it was too late. The driver of the Range Rover adjusted his line to inflict a head-on collision which had a devastating

SUNSET OVER SUNSET © Steve Richards

effect. The Audi's windscreen instantly shattered and both front-seat air-bags deployed. In a heartbeat, three men in black military gear and balaclavas exited the Range Rover. They each went to a different corner of the Audi and shot three rounds from revolvers with silencers into the Audi's stunned occupants before calmly walking back to their car. One paused to reach under the front left wheel arch of the Audi to retrieve a small rectangular tracking device.

The virtually unscathed Range Rover then reversed a short distance before lurching to the left and disappearing down a side street. After thirty seconds, the passenger of the car pulled out a mobile phone and punched in a number.

"Morning has broken," said Shaun into the handset.

"All ok?" came Seamus's reply.

"Enjoyed the second one even more than the first," said Shaun. "Shelling peas." He disconnected, ripped open the back of the phone and threw the SIM card out of the window as the Range Rover sped along the suburban street. The car then suddenly lurched to a halt. Shaun got out and slowly and calmly wandered over to a public litter bin. He posted the mobile as if he was jettisoning a piece of chewing gum and returned to the vehicle.

Craig had insisted that he go to the phone box alone to make the call. He had been over the plan carefully with Clive and Anita, and as long as Pieter was able to play his crucial part, he might have a way out of this. He didn't want to be distracted by people trying to chip in when he was speaking to the police. He called the number he'd been given by Soho CID when he rang earlier to leave his first message.

He hoped the Inspectors were going to take his call. He hoped he had provided enough of a carrot. The phone box just outside Langley Park in near West Wickham was predictably stinky. He wasn't sure if they might trace the call and this box was a good ten minutes' drive from the nearest police station so as long as he kept it short he should be ok if the TV dramas were to be believed.

SUNSET OVER SUNSET © Steve Richards

Clive waited outside the phone box. Craig's heart was racing. On a piece of paper he had written five words to prompt his half of the conversation. The phone itself looked relatively intact. Craig felt a bead of sweat trickle down the middle of his back as he punched in the number.

It connected immediately and, for a second, Craig was startled.

"Hello, you're through to Detective Sergeant Randwick and Inspector Sands of the Soho CID branch of the Metropolitan Police." The voice was loud and confident. "You are on speakerphone. Who am I speaking with, please?"

Craig momentarily froze.

"Hello," he mustered. "I am calling about the murders of a girl and a man the other night. Destiny was the girl's name, well, it was Claire, actually" Craig's nervousness grew as he burbled into the phone. He tried to recover some semblance of order, staring at the words on his piece of paper.

"The victims were both stabbed in the back," he continued. "I was there. Well, I wasn't there when they were murdered. Well, I was, but...."

In the police interview room, Randwick and Sands stared at each other, both raising their eyebrows. Randwick rolled his eyes. Sands butted in, "Sir, please try to slow down and calmly tell us what happened and why you're phoning us."

In the phone box, Craig lowered the piece of paper and closed his eyes. He spoke clearly and slowly.

"Look, I can't tell you my name but I'm guessing you found my DNA at the flat. You won't know who I am because I don't have a criminal record. I followed Destiny home that night and stayed in her spare room. When I woke up next morning, I discovered the bodies and panicked. I fled. I should've called you but I didn't and for that I am unimaginably sorry. After I'd left the flat, I discovered a huge bloodied hunting knife in my overnight bag. I hid it and went to my mum's flat. Since then, I think I've found out, with the help of some others, the identity of the man who committed the murders. He runs a club called The Sunset in Soho and

SUNSET OVER SUNSET © Steve Richards

his name is Seamus Twite. Yesterday, we kidnapped his bar manager by mistake. Today he is going to help us get a confession out of Twite."

Sands and Randwick were now both leaning forward, listening intently. The voice at the other end of the phone had found its thread.

It continued, "Pieter, Twite's bar manager, has bugged his boss's office. He hates him for what he now thinks Twite did to Destiny who he was very fond of. Now I'm planning to go in there today to confront Twite but I'm going to need three things from you." Sands picked up the pen lying on top off his notepad.

"First, I need an assurance that you won't arrest me as soon as I meet you. I realise I'm a prime suspect but I can give you Twite if you allow me to play this out." Craig, still with eyes clamped shut, continued, "Second, my wife, Anita has got a job at the Club. I need you to protect her. She has a part to play in our plan - a crucial part - but you need to protect her at all costs. This mess has nothing to do with her and whatever happens to me, I need to know you will do your utmost to keep her safe."

Sands and Randwick sat motionless apart from Sands' scribbling.

"And finally, and most urgently, I'm going to bring the murder weapon with me. I need you to do some analysis on it straightaway. I realise this might not be a quick job, but I need you to alert your people to be standing by as I'm right on the edge here and I'm not going to sit in a cell to wait for results."

Craig opened his eyes, realising he hadn't heard a sound from the other end of the line. He thought the line might be dead. He checked the credit level on the dial. It flicked downwards to show 50p left by the line was still connected.

After a few more seconds, Sands said, "Tell us where and when to meet you."

"No!" shouted Craig, contorting his face. "I need your assurances on the three conditions before I come anywhere near you." After a second, he added, "Please."

SUNSET OVER SUNSET © Steve Richards

Sands and Randwick looked at each other. "Ok. You have our assurances," uttered Randwick, leaning in towards the speakerphone. "But you're going to need to work with us. This begins with telling us where and when to meet you."

Dave Rushton entered the interview room. Both Randwick and Sands glared at him, Sands lifted an arm to silence Rushton while they listened.

"Outside The Crown and Sceptre pub on Great Titchfield street at 3pm," said Craig.

"We'll be there," asserted Randwick who then disconnected and turned quickly to face Rushton.

"What?!" he barked irritably. "We were in the middle of something, there, Dave, unless you didn't notice."

Rushton was unapologetic. "You're gonna wanna hear this, Sarge," he monotoned. "Four Russians have just been shot dead at a hit and run in Mayfair. It's Dmitri Usanov and his right-hand men. Three men in balaclavas rammed their car, walked over and shot them at point-blank. Purely professional job. Bold as brass. Broad daylight. Several witnesses."

"Fuck me," said Randwick. Sands stared back at Rushton. "That it?" he asked.

"Er, no, as it happens, Inspector," Rushton said to Sands, shifting his weight onto his other foot.

"Donny Blanchard was also murdered this morning. At his house. Single gunshot. Straight through his temple. Through and through. Assassination. His Mrs was upstairs, didn't hear a thing."

"Jesus Fucking Christ," said Randwick.

"It's Twite," said Sands. "Taking out the whole opposition."

"Thanks, Dave," said Randwick to Rushton who exited.

He faced Sands. "What do you reckon? This whole situation is running

SUNSET OVER SUNSET © Steve Richards

away with itself. We've been chasing shadows for two days, playing catch-up all the time. Being played for fools by this Twite fucker..." Sands stared at his shoes, thinking hard.

"I think he'll have been very careful with the Blanchard hit. And it'll probably be hard to tie him to the Usanov thing too. They'll have stolen the car, ditched the guns and ammo, no fingerprints. Balaclavas. He's clever. Sands nodded towards the speakerphone. "This other angle," he said, "might actually be what we need. Again, if he did kill Destiny and her mate in the flat, there will probably be no trace. If this guy does have the knife, it might be useful but it's unlikely to lead us directly and personally to Twite. He's cleverer than that."

You think Twite did Destiny and her friend?" asked Randwick.

"Looks like it," replied Sands. "Surgical incisions. Both bled out according to Gethin. Something personal with this girl. If it was his own handiwork he would have noticed our guy in the spare room and he'd now be on a slab too.

"Unless our guy really did take out Destiny himself?" suggested Randwick without much conviction.

Randwick wearily massaged his temples with his index fingers. He looked back at Sands. "Bet you missed all this," he said wryly. "You've been back ten minutes and walked straight back into World War Three."

Sands thought for a moment. "Ah, well, you know what they say, Dave," said Sands with half a smile. "Good things come to those who wait."

Randwick was glad he wasn't facing this situation without him.

SUNSET OVER SUNSET © Steve Richards

35
Note to Self

Craig told Clive the call had gone as well as can be expected, at least after he'd dropped the script and told it like it was. They both knew there was a good chance he'd be arrested immediately he turned up at the pub. Clive dropped him off at the crematorium and Craig bought a small bunch of flowers from the stall outside the gate.

He wandered toward his father's plot with head bowed, going over the plan to try to reveal any glaring mistakes. Thankfully, the crem' was quiet, with only a couple of old women independently tending to flower arrangements next to different plots. Neither was within a hundred metres of Craig. He knelt by the square memorial stone embedded into the ground and sat back onto his heels on the dry grass.

Craig spoke softly out loud. "Well, you'd have loved this, dad." He looked skywards, then back to the gold lettering which spelt out his dad's name and his notable dates. 'In loving memory' didn't seem to do the depth of feeling justice. It sounded like a cliché to Craig as he read it back, staring at the marble slab, conjuring memories of the man he so desperately wished was there to help him through the toughest 48 hours of his life.

He reached down to touch the cold smooth surface of the stone in an attempt to feel closer and establish a more direct link.

"Can't believe The Euthanasia Brigade kidnapped the wrong bloke." He managed a weak smile and small shake of the head. "This new man Mum's seeing, Dad. He's alright. Treats her well, I think." He paused. "Bit of a posh prick if I'm honest but think you might've actually got on with him in another life."

Craig took a deep breath and relaxed his shoulders. "It's gonna be ok, Dad, isn't it?" Craig felt a warm knot of emotion rise in his chest. A tear dropped from his eye but he wasn't crying. The same had happened at the funeral. Odd. Tears fell steadily as he spoke, in level tone.

SUNSET OVER SUNSET © Steve Richards

"Well, thanks for looking after this for me," Craig lifted the marble slab and retrieved the clear plastic bag, checking around him to see if anyone was watching. "I won't be needing the note now, at least." He replaced the slab.

"Thanks for listening, Dad." 'He rose from his haunches to his knees and stood. "We'll get it right. Don't worry." He kissed the fingers on his right hand then transferred it to the stone. "'Cos if we don't, as Anita says, we're FUCKED."

He secreted the plastic bag under his coat and hurried back to the car smiling to himself.

Sands and Randwick had discussed the plan presented by their earlier caller and decided it was their best option. It wasn't their only option but it was the only one that had the faintest possibility of wrapping up two separate investigations in one. They had spent half an hour debriefing their boss who would have to approve the deployment of the Armed Response Unit.

The recent sudden escalation in violence had created waves in the senior hierarchy and if this civilian was prepared to potentially give them what they needed, it would save lots of time and resources over coming weeks. Because of what had happened to Blanchard and Usanov, Randwick and Sands were provided with two senior 'minders', the Met's best men usually engaged with looking after senior diplomats or Heads of State.

So when they arrived at The Crown and Sceptre pub in advance of their meeting with their mystery caller, Randwick and Sands had a car-full. A separate car-full of armed CID officers was stationed opposite the pub and around the corner an SUV was waiting full of armed police. There was no guarantee this wasn't another ambush given events earlier in the day.

At exactly 3pm, an unremarkable man of average build and height wandered towards the pub accompanied by another man who appeared to be his father. Sands noticed that the senior man walked stiffly,

SUNSET OVER SUNSET © Steve Richards

swinging his arms. Ex-military, he surmised.

The men both stopped outside the pub and the older man checked his watch. The two bodyguards got out of the unmarked car and one then tapped the driver-side window to indicate that Randwick and Sands were cleared to move. The movements were immediately noticed by the older man who nudged the younger man with his shoulder and mumbled something to him.

Randwick and Sands walked towards the two men while the bodyguards scanned the surrounding buildings for anything suspicious. As the two men walked towards them, Craig wasn't filled with confidence. Neither man was physically formidable. They both looked rather scruffy and unkempt, especially compared to Clive's immaculate attire and demeanour.

The policemen came within talking distance and the older man, who Craig assumed was the more senior, said, "Shall we?" and veered off towards a side-street with Craig and Clive obliged to follow.

They wandered fifty metres to a small cafe. As they approached, another man opened the door, speaking into a microphone Craig couldn't see. He didn't look at any of them as they entered but stared over their shoulders, vigilant and alert.

Four cups of black coffee sat steaming on one of the tables. The cafe was empty, commandeered by the police, Craig assumed. They sat. Clive poured some milk from the jug. It was the older policeman who spoke first.

"I'm Detective Sergeant Randwick of Soho CID. This..." he gestured to his right, "is Inspector Nick Sands. We fielded your call earlier. We are also the investigating officers in the unexplained deaths of a man and woman not far from here from stab wounds." Clive was probably used to such stilted, operational conversation. Craig was not.

He replied, emphasising the contrast in tones by adding a smile for artistic impression, "Well, I'm Craig and this is Clive." These policemen were a tough crowd. The younger one, Sands, Craig estimated to be about the same age as him.

SUNSET OVER SUNSET © Steve Richards

"So, Craig," began Sands, "we can go through the fine details of the plan at the station over the next hour or two, but we need to assess if you're in the mental state to pull this off. You've obviously been through a lot in the last day or so." Craig stared at him, mildly affronted.

"We have reason to believe," Randwick said, "that our Mr Twite is at the centre of a spate of gangland killings which culminated this morning in the assassination of one man and the cold-blooded murder of four others."

"I say," exclaimed Clive, who immediately took a sip of his coffee. Randwick continued.

"We have clear reason to believe that we are dealing with a dangerous and totally ruthless man. At present we cannot tie him directly to the murders of the man and woman you discovered around the corner from here, but you need to be under no illusion that this is one professional and utterly ruthless killer."

Craig joined Clive by grasping his own coffee.

Sands spoke next, tag-teaming Randwick. "We need to be 100% sure that you are capable of pulling this off. Several men, including us, will be depending on your actions. And if this morning's anything to go by, Twite is backed up by a team of extremely able men, military-trained."

Clive's moustache twitched. Craig felt the last ounce of confidence drain away. Randwick then rounded off possibly the worst pep talk in history.

"I will not endanger any of the men under my command if we believe for one second that your motives, commitment and abilities are not 100% up to scratch."

Silence reigned. Clive chipped in, "Please remember, officers, that Craig, here, is a civilian with no training."

"That's what we're afraid of," shot back Randwick.

"My point is," continued Clive, "that he's going to need some help, guidance and support. At the moment you're doing a great job of scaring

SUNSET OVER SUNSET © Steve Richards

the life out of him."

"I am here, you know," said Craig defensively. "This is my future we're debating here. I do have a vested interest so please don't talk around me." He lowered his voice and added, "Look, I know I can pull this off. Everyone just needs to play their part. The bar manager said he'd be in very early this morning to bug Twite's office. My wife, Anita, is going to be our extra pair of eyes and ears inside the venue to tip us off about what's going on. You storm the place as soon as we get the evidence we need and we can all be back in that nice pub where we just met for last orders - you're paying."

Inside The Sunset, Pieter had indeed been in earlier than usual. And he had been busy inside Seamus's office. But now he was sat in the main part of the Club with Seamus and his brother, fielding questions about his kidnapping the day before. If Craig thought his interrogation at the cafe was unsympathetic, Seamus and Shaun were making The Spanish Inquisition look like naïve amateurs.

"So you let a couple of old coffin-dodgers bundle you into a sack without a fight?" asked Shaun. He turned to his brother "A man in his prime of life, taken by some OAPs? I'm not buying it, Seamus."

Pieter was rattled. He had been prepared for some awkward questions from his boss, but he didn't know Shaun and the man intimidated him. "They were after you," he said weakly towards Seamus. "I was in your office. They thought I was you."

"Yeah, peas in a pod you two," scoffed Shaun. "Easily mistaken. Peas in a fucking pod."

"Look, I told you before," Pieter pleaded, "they took me to some garage. I was scared. They take me out of the sack and their boss man took one look and knew I was the wrong guy,"

"What did he look like?" asked Seamus. "The boss man?"

"Old guy. Retired military, I think" said Pieter, "like the others."

SUNSET OVER SUNSET © Steve Richards

"How many of them were there, at the warehouse,?" asked Shaun.

"I don't know. Maybe, seven or eight."

Seamus this time: "How did they restrain you?"

"They held my arms. Sat me on a chair."

"What were they wearing?" asked Shaun.

"Er, normal clothes. I didn't really notice." Pieter was wilting under the double-barrelled verbal shotgun.

"Names. Did they use any names?" asked Seamus.

"Er, I'm not sure. Tom? Thomas, maybe?"

"Where did they drop you?" asked Shaun.

"In a street. I told you. In East London. I didn't know it, the area." Pieter reached his palms out towards Seamus. "I told you all this, boss. We should report it to the police, yes?"

"That will be all, Pieter. Go back to your duties." Seamus said, suddenly standing up. He then leaned in close to Pieter's seated position, so close that he could feel Seamus's breath on his face. "But if I find out you're lying to me, Pieter Pyptiuk," he threatened, "I will take great pleasure in slicing you up like that sushi you love so much. And after I've finished with you, I'll be on the first flight out to Poland to fillet some other Pyptiuks."

The questions were over. He straightened up and leaned towards Shaun's right ear. "Office."

The two men walked away and Pieter looked at the impassive faces of Shaun's cohorts. These were grizzled, hard professionals. Pieter scuttled away towards the bar to bottle up for the evening.

As he entered the office, Seamus glanced again at the space where the missing hunting knife should've been. When the door was shut, he

SUNSET OVER SUNSET © Steve Richards

turned to face Shaun. "What do you reckon?"

"He's full o' shite, Seamus," said Shaun dismissively, "You know it as well as I do."

"Yeah. But why? I've worked with the guy for a few years," said Seamus, "He's been solid up to now. No problems. He decides to lie to me after he's been whisked away. Maybe the kidnappers threatened him. Fed him a story to try to get to me."

"Who's he going to side with, Seamus? Who's he going to put his faith in? These ancient old jokers or his boss who he must realise is a nasty bastard. No offence," Shaun held up his hand with a half-smile.

"None taken," said Seamus, dead-pan. "In fact that's probably the nicest thing you've said to me in 20 years."

"So what's the next move?" asked Shaun. "The Russians have been neutralised, the local crew have tragically lost their boss. Do you need us to stick around or can you and your hired help cope from here?"

"Hang around for another 24 hours, Shaun. I'll make it worth your while," said Seamus.

"Aye, ok," said Shaun, "the boys will like the sound of that. Some of those girls you've got working the stage here are a step up from the wifeys they've left at home."

Randwick, Sands and their communications guys were listening in on headsets in the back of a large unmarked van. They had heard every word of the exchange between Seamus and another man. The bug that the bar manager had installed was picking up the dialogue from Seamus's office extremely well.

Sands looked at Randwick, "Still nothing to tie Seamus directly to this morning's killing spree. The other voice must be Shaun Twite, Seamus's older brother. He's now linked, verbally, but we're still going to need Craig to put his head in the lion's mouth."

SUNSET OVER SUNSET © Steve Richards

"And I don't know about you, Nick," said Randwick, "but the lion sounds a little twitchy to me."

"Maybe we wait a day or two for his brother and his mates to bugger off," suggested Sands.

"Well, we could," said Randwick, "but we have ARU signed off for today. And we have this bar manager, Craig and everyone else primed to move today. Best to rattle the lion's cage when we have our people all lined up and before he's got a chance to think."

"One thing we should definitely do," said Sands, "is get our guy's wife to stand down. Otherwise if things go awry she might be getting even more than she bargained for by the sound of it."

36
S. O. S.

Randwick and Sands had a surveillance car outside The Sunset. Since the morning, however, no one had left the club, unless there was a secret exit the police hadn't seen. As the pair made their final preparations, they planned ahead for after the arrest of Seamus and his crew. Spaces were made available at the local holding cells - the terrorist ones at Paddington Green that came with extra security and no sea view.

They considered posting armed guys inside the venue, disguised as punters but after the guy on the front desk had been coshed, they suspected Seamus would be taking no chances and might be searching people on arrival. If armed men were found trying to attend the club, it would immediately scupper the operation.

Anita had indeed been persuaded to call in sick. She spoke to Pieter who played with a straight bat and recorded the absence in the rota, as usual. He didn't flag it to Seamus who trusted Pieter to book the acts and manage his way around unexpected absences. Pieter got the impression that his earlier performance, in the face of the inquisition from Seamus and his cronies, had worked. They didn't appear to suspect him and left him to get on with his duties.

The plan was for Craig to enter the club early evening when it was relatively quiet and the heavy mob were out having a feed. He would demand to speak to the owner, persistently trying to find out information about the death of his friend. He would confront Pieter who would call Seamus to request an audience. There was a good chance Seamus would reject this request. If Craig got difficult and Shaun or Donal were around, there was every chance Craig would be kicked down the stairs. Or worse.

The carrot, to get the audience with Seamus in his office, was the hunting knife. There was a chance Craig would be checked to see if he was wearing a recording device so they couldn't risk an overt 'wire'. However, they already had the bug installed by Pieter so Craig had been

SUNSET OVER SUNSET © Steve Richards

equipped with an inconspicuous panic button sewn into the hem of his jacket. Sands and Randwick would hopefully be following every word of the conversation taking place inside the office. Craig had practised several conversations at the police station to try to get Seamus to implicate himself with any of the murderous activities of the previous 48 hours. Ideally it would be the Destiny killing, letting Craig off the hook. If things went wonky and Craig suddenly needed help, he would press the button and the cavalry would storm the club.

That was the plan; a full confession, several arrests and no one hurt.

After the earlier meeting at the café, Clive had been sent home by the police. It had been decided that his presence wouldn't help. He was offered an expenses-paid taxi home, but he politely declined, pointing out that his car had been left near Holborn the day before and he had to move it before it was towed away.

Craig sat in the back of Randwick's unmarked car, two streets away from The Sunset. It was almost time to rock and roll. Sands was communicating with the two other units stationed in vehicles nearby; a plain-clothes CID team lead by Dave Rushton and Armed Response Team of six men. In total, a dozen police to take down up to nine men in Seamus's crew.

As he sat in silent reflection, Craig started to reconsider the comparative benefits of thirty years in prison. At least in prison you got three meals a day and a colour TV. There was a chance he could be physically attacked by these unmistakeably evil bad guys. If it came to a fight, Craig would try his best but the last actual fight he had was 22 years ago over a stolen Curly-Wurly. At least death would come relatively quickly and he'd side-step a life in prison and the intimate affections of a live-in bearded 'girlfriend' called Bernard.

For the first time, Craig sensed a degree of nervousness among Randwick and Sands. They had been very matter-of-fact and business-like up to now, the embodiments of apathetic professionalism. Now game-time was approaching, Sands' voice was terse and strained. Randwick rapped his fingers anxiously on the steering wheel.

"Ok," said Randwick, turning around to speak to Craig sat diagonally behind him. "It's time."

"Remember," said Sands, "We will be no more than 30 seconds away at all times. Take no chances. Use your panic button if you need to. This operation is a long-shot. The most important thing is for you to come out of there unscathed. You are a material witness if we are able to use more orthodox methods to bring Twite to book."

As Craig got out of the car and walked towards the club entrance, his legs didn't feel connected to his body. He also had an uncontrollably strong urge to laugh out loud. He was five metres away from the front door when the thought popped into his head to walk straight past the entrance and run for the nearest Tube. The mental image of the six armed men in the van round the corner dissuaded him.

Scaling the stairs, Craig noticed there was a different man on the desk at the top of the stairs. He looked meaner, fitter and uglier than the previous man. The man studied Craig disapprovingly the second he walked through the door. He felt the man's eyes bore into him as he walked up the two short flights.

"Er, one, please," said Craig handing forward a ten pound note.

The man stared at him from under a thick monobrow. Both of his hands were under the desk. Craig thought he might be shot dead there and then. A blessed release. After several seconds the man said in a strong Irish accent, "You know the entertainment doesn't start for nearly two hours?"

"Yes, I know," said Craig. "I'm, er, meeting someone here."

The man stared at him again. Craig was convinced he could see into his soul. He touched the outline of the panic button inside the hem of his jacket. The man then suddenly snatched the tenner and said, "Bar's through the doors on the right."

Craig waited for a second then walked inside. He seemed to be the only person there. He wandered up to the bar and noticed for the first time that it was beautifully presented, with decorations of champagne glasses, flowers and bottles tastefully arranged. He also noticed a half-

SUNSET OVER SUNSET © Steve Richards

empty glass display fridge sat on the bar containing what looked like sushi. It was a classier joint than Craig remembered.

Pieter suddenly appeared. As soon as Craig saw him, he could tell that he was in character, a novice method actor enslaved to his craft.

"What can I get you?" he asked, the question dripping with contrived nonchalance. Craig hadn't actually expected that question. Of all the questions to ask someone standing at a bar. Craig wasn't actually expecting any questions at all.

His mind raced. Does he mean it? Is he expecting me to order a drink to maintain the pretence? Should I actually order one? Have I got any money on me? Should it be an alcoholic drink or might that impair my faculties? If I order a soft drink will it look suspicious? If I order an alcoholic drink should I order a bottle because it might make a useful weapon? I wonder if they have Moretti, that's my favourite? So many questions flashed through Craig's mind in less than two seconds.

Pieter prompted his customer by raising his eyebrows and keeping them there. Craig glanced at Pieter into one of the fridges behind his barman's knees.

"Beck's please, mate."

Craig then realised that Seamus would probably have a CCTV feed of the bar in his office. As planned, he asked Pieter if he could speak to the boss. Pieter dutifully declined, pretence maintained. Craig than reeled off his lines, insisting he speak to the boss and Pieter picked up the phone behind the bar.

"Boss, I've got a guy here wants to speak to you."

Seamus replied, "I know, I can see him. He's the guy who was in with his father the other day, asking about Destiny. What does he want?"

"He wants another chat." Pieter said, glancing round at Craig who was tapping the top of his beer bottle as if drumming out the beat to the music that was softly playing in the background.

SUNSET OVER SUNSET © Steve Richards

"And you've told him to fuck off, I take it...?" asked Seamus laconically into his phone handset while watching the bar's live feed on the laptop sat on his desk.

"Of course," said Pieter, swinging his head back towards the champagne display, away from Craig. "I was going to get the guy from the front desk to help me to throw him out but then he mentioned something odd so that's why I am calling you."

"And..." prompted Seamus.

"Well," Pieter continued, "he is claiming to know the whereabouts of the hunting knife that's missing from the cabinet in your office."

"Is he now...?" said Seamus, playfully intrigued but not sounding in the least bit worried. "If he's genuine, he's got some bollocks walking in here, wanting to front me up." There was a pause.

"Shall I show him in, boss?" asked Pieter.

"No," Seamus replied and Pieter immediately closed his eyes and winced, just as Craig glanced over at him. The knot in Craig's stomach added another twist.

"Let him sip his beer for a few moments. Shaun, Donal and the boys will be back soon from their dinner so I'll see him when they get back. Tell him to wait, the cheeky wee fucker." He disconnected immediately.

Pieter wandered slowly back to Craig and told him the news. Craig sipped at his beer. Pieter said, "Look, we need to push it or the heavy mob will be back soon. Time to get creative."

Craig took a long swig of his beer from the bottle as Pieter turned away from him to busy himself behind the bar. Craig needed to force the issue. Time was running out.

"Look here," he said aggressively in Pieter's general direction, his voice echoing around the empty club. "I'm not here to see a fucking dentist. You can't keep me hanging around. I need to see the boss man and I need to see him now!" He immediately regretted the dentist reference.

SUNSET OVER SUNSET © Steve Richards

He had a lot to learn in the 'menacing language' stakes.

Pieter threw his hands up theatrically to try to defuse Craig's mood.

"And don't give me any more bullshit!" shrieked Craig. He was now in for a proverbial penny. "You call the fucker back now or I'm going to march over there," he said pointing, "to his office." As soon as he said it, he shrank. He realised he shouldn't know where the office was. But he was interrupted by a voice behind him.

"A lot of commotion for one so alone and slightly built," said Seamus. Craig swung round to face him, tightening the grip on his bottle in his hand.

Seamus continued, amused by the obvious naivety of the prey stood in front of him. "Pieter here tells me you want to talk to me about knives."

"Well, er, yes, in a matter of fact. I do," insisted Craig, jutting out his chin. Pieter stopped polishing the glass he was holding.

"We had better adjourn to my office, then," said Seamus, walking away from Craig who looked at Pieter then turned to hurry after his target.

SUNSET OVER SUNSET © Steve Richards

37
Just Shootin' the Breeze

Randwick and Sands, sitting in the car outside the venue were both wearing mics with earpieces linked to the bug in Seamus's office. As soon as they heard the door swing open, they both put their index fingers to their ears to concentrate on the dialogue to follow.

"All units," said Randwick. "Standing by. Suspect in play."

As he swaggered round to take his seat at the far side of the huge mahogany desk, Seamus seemed in the mood to toy with his would-be interrogator. He had obviously sized up his combatant, physically and mentally, and didn't seem the least bit worried.

"Firstly, let me admire your balls," said Seamus, waving an arm to usher Craig into the seat opposite. "They must be huge to come in here and front me up. Either that or you were a VERY close friend of our poor dear-departed Destiny. As a feisty girl herself, I would dare say she would be a big fan of your spunk, to use an Americanism."

Craig didn't have a clue what to say. He leaned forward to put his bottle on the desk in front of him. He gathered his wits and remembered the cues that Randwick and Sands had been through with him.

"Mr Twite..." he began, only to be immediately interrupted.

"Seamus! Please call me Seamus. And you are...?"

"Er, Craig,"

Outside in the car, Sands looked at Randwick. The former raised his left eyebrow, the latter started shaking his head slowly.

"Well, Craig, let's get on with it as I'm expecting my brother any minute. He's a guy who would LOVE to meet you."

SUNSET OVER SUNSET © Steve Richards

Craig tried to rally. "I'm happy to get to the point if you let me get a fucking word in edgeways."

Listening intently, Randwick and Sands both gave a synchronised wince. Craig pushed on.

"I think you killed my friend Destiny. Or you had her killed. I've no idea why, but I happened to be in the flat the night she was murdered. When I woke up I discovered the bodies of her and an unknown man. I panicked and fled. Then I found a blood-stained knife in my overnight bag. I almost threw it in the Thames but didn't get a chance so I stashed it instead."

Seamus stared him down, still with a look of smug amusement across his features.

"I was also very fond of Destiny," the Irishman said. "She was a good girl, a good worker and gorgeous too. A sensational body as I'm sure you will have noticed, Craig." He leaned forward and placed both hands facing downwards on the edge of the desk, thumbs disappearing underneath. "I too am keen to understand the identity of her killer. And when I do, if I get to them before the police, and I usually do, I will be sorely tempted to exact a terrible revenge."

"So how do you explain the disappearance of one of your knife collection?" said Craig swinging round to his right and waving his right arm in the direction of the cabinet on the wall.

"Another mystery, Craig," said Seamus, his hands still immobile on the desk.

"I have passed the suspected murder weapon to the police," said Craig, "who have carried out tests on the knife I found in my bag. Your fingerprints are on it."

"Of course they are," confirmed Seamus. "I put the knife in the cabinet myself. I still don't know what this possibly has to do with me," he added.

"I wanted to come here today before the police arrest you to ask you 'why?'," said Craig shifting forward in his seat, closer to Seamus. "Why would you murder a sweet and hard-working girl? There was no forced

SUNSET OVER SUNSET © Steve Richards

entry so as her employer and patron of her photo shoots, no doubt you'll have had a key to her flat. Someone entered the flat, murdered her in cold blood then tried to frame me by planting the knife."

Craig was getting frustrated at the lack of antagonism he was able to trigger in the man sat opposite. Time to up the pace.

"She actually mentioned you fondly," said Craig, "as a man she respected." Seamus wasn't biting so Craig raised the volume. "So tell me WHY you fucker!" he shouted, reinforcing the final word by banging his fist on the desk.

At precisely the same moment, outside The Sunset Club a large black Audi Q7 pulled up and four men jumped out, one from the front and three from the back. Sands spotted them before Randwick who was tuned into the conversation going on in his ear. Sands instinctively knew trouble had arrived and he waved at Randwick to point them out.

Over the mic Sands said with urgency, "Armed assailants walking towards The Sunset." Randwick recognised the person leading the gang of men; a young well-dressed slim man in his late 20s holding a handgun.

"Fuck," said Randwick. "It's Donald Blanchard."

As the newly arrived foursome approached the club entrance, from the opposite direction Shaun, Donal and their crew of Irishmen marched towards them bound for the same destination. Sands and Randwick watched in horror as they drew closer to each other realising what was about to unfold.

"Armed units," shouted Sands urgently into his mic, "Go. Repeat GO!"

As Donald and Shaun got closer, it became clear to both of them in just a few strides that there would be a clash. Undeterred, Donald kept his pace steady, raised the gun in his right hand to shoulder height and fired. Shaun took the bullet in his shoulder and he immediately hit the pavement. There were screams from the few people who were on the same street at the loud bang. As one, they instinctively crouched and tried to take cover.

As the first shot rang out, its sound reverberating and echoing off the buildings on either side of the narrow road, both crews darted towards the cover provided by the row of parked cars. The Irishmen had a clear numerical advantage and one of Shaun's men ran up to his prone body, grabbed him under each arm from behind and dragged him back along the pavement, pulling him into the gutter. Several shots were exchanged and more screams from bystanders rang out.

Randwick and Sands were now out of the car and taking cover with their minders behind a post-box. They were directly opposite the club and could see both crews, the Irishmen to their left and the Blanchards to their right, crouching down between and behind the cars. Several more shots rang out, some from a hand-held machine gun from their right. The noise was deafening. At least two car alarms squealed to add to the cacophony.

Despite pushing his earpiece into his head, Sands could hear nothing of the conversation going on inside The Sunset so he removed it. Glass shattered and bullets fizzed and exploded as they riddled the cars.

Another of Shaun's men was hit and he lay down in the street. Within seconds a van screeched around the corner and pulled up in the middle of the road directly between the two crews. Six men poured out of a side door towards Randwick and Sands, on the opposite side to the gun battle. The Armed Response Unit men took cover, crouching behind their vehicle. Their leader, who was also wearing a headset, looked to Randwick and Sands for direction.

Randwick made a mime like he was doing the breast-stroke. Three men fanned out to either end of the van. Some bullets were fired into the van from the left hand side but they ricocheted off with bright sparks splintering in all directions. The van was obviously equipped with bullet-proof glass and armour plating, providing an effective shield.

One of Donald's men then hit the deck, holding his neck. Sands could see blood pouring from the wound. Donald looked down at the man for a second or two then continued firing at the other gang.

Randwick shouted into his phone calling for back-up. This was getting uglier by the second.

SUNSET OVER SUNSET © Steve Richards

Inside the fully sound-proofed Sunset Club, Pieter, as planned, was poised outside the door to Seamus's office. He leant his ear to the door and could hear muffled voices. He then heard Craig shout the word 'Why!" which was his cue to enter.

As Pieter walked in, Seamus stared up from his seat behind the desk and greeted him with all the cordial respect of a cobra greeting a mongoose.

"What the fuck do you want?" he spat.

"I heard raised voices, Boss, that's all," said Pieter. "I thought you might need some help. Shaun and the boys are still not back from the cafe." As he spoke he walked towards Seamus, standing to his left, behind the opposite side of the desk from Craig. The news about Shaun was a pre-ordained signal to Craig that time had not completely run out.

Seamus's hands had not moved from the desk, palms down, thumbs underneath.

"I'm still waiting for my answer," barked Craig. His hand ached from banging his fist on the stone-like slab of mahogany.

Seamus glared at Craig but directed his words at Pieter.

"This wee cunt here, Pieter, this WEE CUNT has marched in here to tell me I murdered Destiny and that he has the murder weapon with my prints on it to prove it. Can you BELIEVE the bollocks on this kid, Pieter. Unbe-FUCKING-lievable!"

Craig noticed that as the volume of Seamus's voice increased, so a purple rash emerged from his neck-line of his smart dark blue polo shirt, creeping up to colour his face. As the volume and profanity of Seamus's rhetoric increased, Craig fingered the outline of the panic button in his coat lining. Pieter shifted slightly, moving closer to Seamus but further behind him, out of his eye-line.

"I'm not leaving here without an explanation," insisted Craig, raising his own voice to try to match the man opposite him.

"And he doesn't even shut up," Seamus continued, still addressing

SUNSET OVER SUNSET © Steve Richards

Pieter, "he just keeps pointing the finger and shouting the odds." He shifted slightly forward in his chair, his eyes fixed on Craig. His face was now fully flushed. He was about to blow his top. He dropped the pitch of his next sentence to conjure the most menacing tone Craig had ever heard directed at him.

"Now you listen to me, ya wee prick, and you listen good," growled Seamus. "I am not in the habit of murdering defenceless women. I don't know who the fuck you are, or what you're trying to prove here, but I will tell you this: if you EVER set foot in my club again, or if I EVER clap eyes on you again, I will cut you to pieces myself. Now, if you've got an ounce of common sense, you will stand up and walk quickly out of this office. Final chance."

"You just don't get it, do you?" Craig said, holding his nerve. "You are a classic bully. You're not even listening to me. I'm in the frame for these murders. My life is fucking over. And you sit there threatening me, you cocky cunt." Craig shuffled forward in his seat and put his palms on the table to mirror Seamus's pose. Pieter was now standing almost directly behind him.

"I want you to admit you had Destiny murdered," shouted Craig, "and I want you to tell me WHY!"

"I tried to warn you," Seamus said softly and then pressed the button under the desk with his thumb.

Nothing happened. Perplexed, Seamus pressed again with his thumb, harder.

Craig immediately put his own thumb under the edge of his side of the desk and pressed the button that Pieter had installed earlier that morning. Seamus watched uncomprehendingly and felt Pieter's arms clamp down on his shoulders at the exact moment a sharp jolt of electricity crackled up through his body. Seamus was wracked with pain.

Craig released the button for a second. "Just admit it!" he shouted then pressed the button again, holding it down to cause Seamus's body to convulse in spasms, his face contorted in agony. Craig also screwed up his features as he kept the button depressed.

SUNSET OVER SUNSET © Steve Richards

Pieter shouted, "Craig! Enough!" over the top of Seamus's guttural howl but Craig kept the button depressed. "Craig!" Pieter screamed, "You'll kill him!!" and took his hands off Seamus's shoulders to release him. Pieter threw Seamus from the chair. He lay on the carpet, moaning.

"Jesus Christ, Craig," said Pieter, "Two second bursts, we agreed. I told you! Three seconds maximum!" He bent down to look at Seamus who had curled into the foetal position. Craig hurried round the desk. Seamus was motionless but emitting a low, groaning sound.

"Still no fucking confession," Craig said with no hint of regret. He then swung his right foot and kicked Seamus hard in the groin.

"Are you out of your fucking mind?!" Pieter shrieked. He stepped over Seamus's prone body to stand in front of Craig to prevent a repeat.

Outside the club, the shooting had become more sporadic. Ammunition levels were low. The armed police had not shot at any of the gang members because they had their sights set on each other. One of the armed police had retrieved a loud haler from inside the vehicle and he was appealing to both sets of men to hold their fire and drop their weapons. The police then extracted riot shields from the van and fanned out either side of the vehicle.

Randwick and Sands were focused most keenly on Donald Blanchard who was in no mood to comply with any instructions. As the teams of three armed police walked slowly towards each gang behind their bullet-proof shields, with the loud haler ringing out behind them, Donald made a bolt from the parked cars across the pavement towards the front door of the club. The remaining Irishmen took pot shots at him but failed to bring him down.

Shaun then bolted from the line of cars and ran towards the club. He couldn't afford Donald to get there first and have the jump on Seamus. As Shaun reached the door just before his foe, a bullet from one of the Blanchard crew hit him in the same shoulder as his previous wound. He hit the deck again hard and didn't move. An instant later, Donald skipped over Shaun's body, and reached across to open the club's door

SUNSET OVER SUNSET © Steve Richards

towards him. As he ran around it to the left to enter the stairway inside, he was exposed to the enemy's line of fire for a split second, but just enough for a round to hit him in the knee. He yelped but managed to dive inside and the door shut behind him. The Irishmen peppered the door with bullets, riddling it with holes.

By now the armed police were almost on top of both gangs. Randwick and Sands broke cover and ran across the road, making sure they remained behind the line of protection provided by the riot shields. The two remaining active members of Blanchard's gang capitulated first, their leader gone and their appetite for further carnage assuaged.

They dropped their weapons and held up their arms. Having seen this, the Irishmen looked at each other then slowly put down their weapons. They too were without their leader, slumped just outside the club door, motionless apart from a slight twitching from the arm connected to his injured shoulder.

A police helicopter now roared overhead. Sands quickly repositioned his ear-piece. Sands turned to Randwick. "Panic button deployed," he said urgently. "We need to get inside that club!"

Upstairs in The Sunset, Pieter and Craig stared at each other. Neither knew what to do next. Seamus lay prone on the floor. Craig pressed his panic button. "30 seconds, they said," said Craig. "I've had enough of this."

They both exited the office and walked uncertainly back towards the bar. More seconds passed.

"Where the fuck are they?" said Craig.

"That's way more than 30 seconds," Pieter observed. "Seamus is going to go mental when he recovers." The door to the main room then burst open and a man neither of them recognised limped in. He immediately pointed his gun at both Craig and Pieter who both dived over the top of the bar to take cover, crashing down the other side in two heaps.

SUNSET OVER SUNSET © Steve Richards

"Where is he?" screamed the man in a strong Cockney accent, firing off a round that shattered the sushi fridge above Pieter and Craig who were showered in glass. They looked at each other in terror.

"Where is he!?" repeated the voice moving closer. Huddled behind the bar, Pieter and Craig looked around in vain to find anything they could use as a weapon. Before they could grab anything, the face of a man in his late 20s loomed over them from across the bar.

"Where is the fucker?" the man implored, saliva dripping from his mouth, his face bathed in sweat.

"Office," said Pieter meekly, pointing over in the right direction. Donald immediately turned around and lurched away, his right arm outstretched in front of him at shoulder height, handgun pointing the way.

Back behind the bar, Craig pressed the panic button again and again. Still no cavalry. Pieter and Craig both got to their feet and, crouched, peeked over the top of the bar to watch Donald reach the corridor leading to the office and scream, "I'm gonna fucking end you, Irish! You murdered my facking Dad, you..." but the last word was muffled as Donald disappeared into the office.

Craig and Pieter expected to hear a bang as Seamus was put out of his misery. Instead, Donald burst back out of the office after a few seconds and limped back towards the bar, his gun still pointing the way.

"Right you two cants!" he shouted. "I'm gonna ask you one last time," he lurched quickly towards them.

Over Donald's shoulder as he approached, Craig and Pieter suddenly saw the middle of stage curtain twitch. Seamus appeared, pointing his own gun at the back of Donald's head as he crossed the floor.

Donald opened his mouth again to speak but his words were drowned out by a huge explosion of noise as Seamus fired.

Craig expected to see Donald fall but the bullet narrowly missed him and he swung round to see who was firing at him. Craig heard a noise to his right and Pieter slumped back down behind the bar. He lay on

SUNSET OVER SUNSET © Steve Richards

his back and Craig saw he'd been hit in the top of the chest, just below his neck. His white t-shirt was quickly turning crimson. Behind him, Donald pointed his gun at Seamus and they both fired simultaneously. Seamus was hit in the right arm causing the gun he was holding in that hand to shoot across the stage. He slumped to one knee, covering his wound with his left hand. Donald, still remarkably unscathed by either of Seamus's bullets, walked slowly towards him.

"Right, you Irish bastard, now it's my turn to turn on the juice." He pointed the gun upwards towards the stage, aiming for Seamus's head. Craig turned his gaze from Pieter to events unfolding across the floor.

"You treated me like a naughty school-kid in your office," said Donald, his voice slightly lowered. "Then you assassinated my dad." He wiped his brow with his sleeve. "Now this naughty school kid is going to take everything from you."

From the corner of Craig's eye from his position crouched behind the bar, he saw the main door to the club swing silently open. A man dressed in black lifted a pistol and fired. Across the main floor, Donald's head jerked violently to the right and he sank immediately to the floor like a marionette with its strings suddenly cut.

Seamus, open-mouthed, looked over towards his brother.

"You always were a lousy shot," Shaun said, then slumped onto a chair before wobbling and falling forward to the floor. Seamus stood back up and walked towards his brother, jumping down from the stage.

Craig looked back towards Pieter who was lying on his back, staring skywards. He knelt beside him. Pieter's mouth was moving, trying to talk. It was a mere whisper. Craig leaned forward over him, lowering his right ear towards Pieter's twitching mouth.

"Craig," he rasped "forgive me." Craig lifted his head to look round at Pieter. "Don't worry," Craig said, "it wasn't your fault."

Pieter's mouth moved and Craig lowered his ear.

"Craig..." Pieter said, his voice barely audible, "but it was, you see. It was my fault. I killed Destiny." Craig didn't move his ear but his eyes widened.

"Craig, I killed her," Pieter rasped, "I loved her. But she...," his voice failed as he swallowed, a gurgling noise coming from his throat. Craig raised his head and looked into Pieter's eyes. He was drowning in his own blood. Another mouth twitch and Craig again lowered his ear. "She didn't love me. She wouldn't love me, Craig. She loved another. He was there that night." Pieter blinked, his eye-lashes brushing Craig's ear.

"I couldn't take it anymore," Pieter whispered, "The rejection. I loved her and I couldn't watch her love another. Seamus is a bastard. So I tried to frame him by taking the knife from his case. You...were....unlucky..."

Craig felt a warm breath on his neck as Pieter exhaled for the last time. Craig looked at Pieter, his lifeless eyes still open. As he stood, unsteadily, back to his feet. He noticed a row of sushi knives on a granite chopping board to the left of a row of raw fish. Both were covered in shattered glass.

The door to the club was pushed open by a riot shield and a loud haler announced, "Armed police, put down your weapons!"

The riot shield encroached into the pub. Seamus, kneeling beside his brother who was unconscious on the floor, looked over at Craig, his mouth gaping open.

Sands and Randwick shuffled in behind the shield. They quickly saw the danger was over and they hurried over to Craig.

"You hurt?" said Randwick urgently, looking past him to Pieter's body behind the bar. Sands shook Craig by the elbow. "Craig, are you ok?"

Craig blinked and then looked straight at Sands. "It was Pieter. Pieter was left-handed."

EPILOGUE

Craig travelled back to the police station in the back of the car driven by Sands. He was dazed and silent. When he arrived back, Anita, Clive and his mum were there to meet him. Anita and his mum embraced him together, hugging him tightly. When they finally broke, Clive leaned forward and shook his hand vigorously. "Well done, young man. Thoroughly fine job," he said keenly.

The fingerprint taken from Pieter's lifeless body matched the print on the crucifix on the dead man in Destiny's flat. It was the evidence that sealed his guilt. He was left-handed, Seamus was not.

Seamus readily confirmed to the police that Pieter was jealous of his fond relationship with Destiny. He admitted that he treated Pieter with contempt, although he was quick to add that he didn't discriminate, he treated most people similarly. He also was happy to divulge that Pieter had been the one to wire up the electric chair in his office but he was quick to add that it was for amusement purposes only.

Randwick and Sands also learned that Pieter was an expert sushi chef so when his hatred of Seamus boiled over and his jealousy became unbearable, he saw an opportunity to replicate the surgical nature of Seamus's alleged murders to try to frame his boss. The hunting knife probably wasn't the murder weapon after all.

Pieter's mistake had been to ignore the guest bedroom. He had assumed the holdall belonged to Destiny's lover and planted the knife there to avoid carrying a bloodied murder weapon around Soho at midnight. If Craig had not been anaesthetised so effectively by the ouzo, he would have stirred and interrupted Pieter, with fatal consequences.

The irony was certainly not lost on Craig when he realised that despite all the government health warnings, drinking lots of strong alcohol had almost certainly saved his life. He told Sands he planned to stay down south with Anita for the rest of the weekend then fly back up to Edinburgh. The whole ordeal had seemed to cement their relationship.

They would be required to provide evidence when the case came to trial. Craig confirmed Pieter's shooting had been accidental and Seamus was firing in self-defence.

In quiet reflection under the fluorescent lights of the station, Craig thought back to when they'd inadvertently kidnapped Pieter and had him surrounded in the chair. He remembered Pieter's reaction when they told him Destiny was dead. His surprise was convincing and now he realised that the sadness of her death was heart-felt. Now he'd had some time to think, Craig also recalled that Pieter mentioned the 'stabbing' although no one had mentioned a knife up until that point.

Sands admired Craig's perceptiveness and said he might have made a decent Copper in another life.

As Sands made a chronological list of events since his return to work, he hoped Seamus would forgive Craig for electrocuting him in his office, given the circumstances, and not come after him for petty retribution. Sands thought it unlikely but he had learned to expect the unexpected when it came to Seamus Twite.

Sands finally drove home at 2am. Basic details of the gun battle in central London were covered in the news bulletin squawking from his car radio as he drove. All he could think about was his son. He would savour their trip to the cricket at the weekend.

As he weaved through the deserted streets, Sands suspected Seamus would emerge from this recent carnage unscathed. His brother, Shaun, would recover from his wounds but face prosecution for the gun battle. One of his henchmen would probably take the rap for killing the Blanchard gang member in the street battle and his killing of Donald would probably be downgraded to manslaughter. Sands entertained the rather depressing thought that Shaun Twite would likely be released in less than three years.

Sands expected Seamus Twite would move quickly and efficiently to fill the power vacuum left by the demises of Donny, his son and Dmitri Usanov. Sands knew he would commit himself tirelessly to work with Randwick to bring Twite down eventually. The thought was accompanied by a dull echo of pain from the scar on his back. Seamus Twite was a

SUNSET OVER SUNSET © Steve Richards

menace and Sands knew he and his family would not be safe until he was finally snared.

For now, though, Sands mulled over the events of the previous two days and felt glad he'd gone back to work. His involvement had directly helped to clear an innocent man.

The news bulletin on the car radio gave way to a song Sands recognised. As he flashed through the fading lights of central London towards the suburbs, Sands hummed along quietly to an old soul tune by Howard Melville who crooned, 'Don't leave me this way...''

Seamus Twite, John Randwick and Nick Sands
will return in the sequel, **Blood Red Sunset.**

SUNSET OVER SUNSET © Steve Richards

About the author:

Steve Richards is a Londoner who moved to Scotland with his family in 2008. He now speaks Glaswegian.

He has been an MD of a couple of marketing agencies for 20 years or so where he has nurtured and refined his natural talents for bullshit and swearing.

Some of the content of this book is semi-autobiographical (most dreams are, after all). For instance, the author plays poker but he has never tortured anyone to death with a scalpel. Not yet, anyway.

This is his first novel but he hopes to write more and a sequel, **Blood Red Sunset**, will be available early in 2015.

SUNSET OVER SUNSET © Steve Richards

SUNSET OVER SUNSET © Steve Richards

SUNSET OVER SUNSET © Steve Richards